SPECIAL MESSAGE TO READERS

This book is published under the auspices of

THE ULVERSCROFT FOUNDATION

(registered charity No. 264873 UK)

Established in 1972 to provide funds for research, diagnosis and treatment of eye diseases. Examples of contributions made are: —

A Children's Assessment Unit at
Moorfield's Hospital, London.

•

Twin operating theatres at the
Western Ophthalmic Hospital, London.

•

A Chair of Ophthalmology at the
Royal Australian College of Ophthalmologists.

•

The Ulverscroft Children's Eye Unit at the
Great Ormond Street Hospital For Sick Children,
London.

You can help further the work of the Foundation by making a donation or leaving a legacy. Every contribution, no matter how small, is received with gratitude. Please write for details to:

**THE ULVERSCROFT FOUNDATION,
The Green, Bradgate Road, Anstey,
Leicester LE7 7FU, England.
Telephone: (0116) 236 4325**

**In Australia write to:
THE ULVERSCROFT FOUNDATION,
c/o The Royal Australian and New Zealand
College of Ophthalmologists,
94-98, Chalmers Street, Surry Hills,
N.S.W. 2010, Australia**

THE MAVERICKS

Despite his innocence, Adam Ballard had served eight years in prison. On release he returns to the Texas cattle ranch where he grew up. But his father is dead and his stepmother has remarried, and the past and present have entwined in a web of violence. Drawn into a bitter rivalry where guns blaze and men are lynched, Adam's past is part of the jigsaw of double-dealing, murder . . . and *mavericking*, the illegal branding of other men's cattle . . .

*Books by Mark Bannerman
in the Linford Western Library:*

ESCAPE TO PURGATORY
THE EARLY LYNCHING
MAN WITHOUT A YESTERDAY
THE BECKONING NOOSE
GRAND VALLEY FEUD
RENEGADE ROSE
TRAIL TO REDEMPTION
COMANCHERO RENDEZVOUS
THE PINKERTON MAN
RIDE INTO DESTINY
GALVANIZED YANKEE
RAILROADED!
THE FRONTIERSMAN
LUST TO KILL
HOG-TIED HERO
BLIND TRAIL
BENDER'S BOOT
LEGACY OF LEAD
FURY AT TROON'S FERRY
GUNSMOKE AT ADOBE WALLS

MARK BANNERMAN

THE MAVERICKS

Class
No.

Alloc.

ULV

North Somerset Library
and Information Service

1 2 0375852 3

Complete and Unabridged

LINFORD
Leicester

First published in Great Britain in 2007 by
Robert Hale Limited
London

First Linford Edition
published 2008
by arrangement with
Robert Hale Limited
London

The moral right of the author has been asserted

Copyright © 2007 by Anthony Lewing
All rights reserved

British Library CIP Data

Bannerman, Mark
  The mavericks.—Large print ed.—
Linford western library
1. Western stories
2. Large type books
I. Title
823.9'14 [F]

ISBN 978–1–84782–279–6

Published by
F. A. Thorpe (Publishing)
Anstey, Leicestershire

Set by Words & Graphics Ltd.
Anstey, Leicestershire
Printed and bound in Great Britain by
T. J. International Ltd., Padstow, Cornwall

This book is printed on acid-free paper

This book is dedicated to the inspiration of such great Western authors as *Will Henry* and *Elmer Kelton* — and also to my grandson and fellow writer *Jordan Catto*.

1

Adam Ballard felt tension running through his broad shoulders as he gazed down into the mile-wide valley where he had grown up. He had reined in his stocking-legged bay horse, halted for a moment, glad enough for the respite after the long hours of his night-ride. He was scarcely visible amid the mottled shadows of the hill-slope spruce. He wore the new white linen shirt and Levis especially purchased for his homecoming. His dust-coloured Stetson was pulled low over his steel-grey eyes but it did not conceal the unease which showed in his bearded face. As if for reassurance, he touched the twelve-gauge shotgun nestled in its scabbard beneath his knee.

The Ballard family had come to this valley in the late 1840s and by this time the two children had been born and

John Ballard had become widowed, having lost his wife to a fever. He had re-married Hannah Briggs, an austere lady who had never shown real love to Adam but seemed to resent him.

It was a peaceful July morning here in the sawgrass country of Southern Texas, with jays flashing in brilliant arcs and the heat not yet risen. The beauty of the valley had remained undimmed in Adam's memory, fringed as it was on the west by rock-crested hills. But now his gaze swung to the ranch house. During his childhood the family had scraped a living breeding hogs and chickens, ploughing and planting their crops in the meadows, hunting the adjacent thickets for the meat and hides they needed, thankful that they were within bucket-carrying distance of the river. But gradually Adam's father, Will Ballard, had become aware of the vast, untapped wealth that was on his doorstep. It lay within the mysterious, evil-thorned *brasada*, the seemingly endless wilderness of brushland, irregularly cleaved by streams that spread northwards.

Here, on the upper Trinity River, riches could be made by chasing down the wild Spanish cattle which grazed along the countless streams of the thicketed pastures. This was the greatest natural breeding refuge for feral cattle ever known. The high-withered, curly-haired beasts had gone unbranded by men since the sixteenth century — the days of the *conquistadors*. Now, demand for hides was growing on the northern markets. It seemed that all a man needed to be in business was a fleet mustang, a strong riata and a powerful gun. And as time went on it became evident that the cattle were valuable not only for their skins but also for their meat.

Will Ballard had dreamed of the future, imagining a prosperous ranch to replace their meagre doghouse shacks. And he would have realized his dreams had death not cut him down, eight years since, at the age of fifty-two.

He had been murdered, shot through the head. And Adam had been charged with the crime, placed on trial and sentenced to imprisonment. Only his youth had saved him from the rope. Now he had served his time, eight years, and he had earned his release.

At sixteen, when he had commenced his sentence, he'd left behind not only his freshly bereaved stepmother, Hannah, and his fifteen-year-old sister Altha, but the first structurings of the ranch envisaged by his father. Now, the sturdy-built spread, the Double-X, had grown beyond the recognition, with its collection of hide-sheds, barns, log bunkhouses and polecorrals, not to mention the fine house, with its massive timbers flanked by wings of fieldstone. Across the surrounding meadows long-horned cattle were grazing and in the distance he could see the dark beginnings of the great *brasada* with its mesquite trees, heavy with beans, and black chaparral stretching, it seemed, to the end of the world.

The Texas legislature had passed a law whereby hides would not be accepted at market unless they bore the brand of the seller. Now, it was common knowledge that unscrupulous men, so-called maverickers, cow-stealers, were venturing into the brushlands, branding unscrupulously, caring little for the true ownership.

Adam had received no communication from his family during his years of incarceration. He had been completely disowned by his stepmother.

For the first three months of his freedom he had worked on a farm in Louisiana, labouring to earn sufficient money to establish some sort of independence. He purchased an ivory-gripped Remington Army Revolver .44 with the barrel cut down and, for want of something better to do, spent his evenings practising with it, improving his handling and aim.

Now freshly fitted out, mounted on a good horse and armed, he was back to confront the ghosts of his past.

He had broadened out from the

5

callow youth he had been at the time of his father's death. Beneath the brim of his hat his hair showed the same bronze that had always been the hallmark of the Ballard clan, somehow synonymous with the fiery temper and sense of avenging perceived wrongs that had filtered down from their Scottish forebears. The hard prison life, the brutal toil on the chain-gang, had toughened him, bulking his muscles. It had also strengthened his resolve to return home.

He knew that the sweat of other men had turned the Double-X Ranch into its current affluence, and he was sure that his stepmother, despite her bereavement, would have overseen the expansion. He dreaded facing her again, also his sister Altha. What changes would the years have brought to them? And there was one other whom he dreaded meeting, the man who had previously been his father's foreman — Seth Hardeman. He had no confirmation that Hardeman was still in the employ of the Ballards, but he suspected that it was he who had contrived the prosperity of the spread, had somehow taken the place of his father. A stab of jealously had Adam pursing his lips.

Yes, Adam Ballard had left for prison disgraced and shamed, knowing that his stepmother would have shed no tears had the judge sentenced him to the rope. Now he took a deep breath, touched his heels to the bay's flanks and emerged from the shadows, riding down at a misleadingly casual pace into the valley.

He was coming home. But what awaited him?

★　★　★

Early on the day prior to Adam Ballard's return, Seth Hardeman with a party of five Double-X cowhands, Bilson, Pommer, Sterner, Seymour and Batty, had left the ranch and headed into the *brasada*, taking with them the necessary irons required for branding.

Their legs were encased in leather brush-chaps, black and greasy. They were mounted upon the small, wiry mustangs that were ideal for moving through the vast confusion of sunless copses that separated the open, bright-skied savannas. Numerous calves had been born and now, while they stayed close to their mothers, was the time to mark them with the Double-X brand, but it was hard and dangerous work catching them and avoiding the vicious horns of their parents. The Texas Longhorns truly lived up to their reputation and would pinion a man at the smallest incitement. Not only did the calf have to be immobilized but so did the indignant mother who did not appreciate her offspring being tampered with.

Seth Hardeman was a hard man with a dour mouth. There was a chastening light in his dark eyes and a fierce stare which forced those who opposed him to back down. He was big-boned, hard-working, determined, and he had given

Hannah Ballard the strength she had needed after her husband's death. He had shared Will Ballard's ambition, his drive, and had stepped into his shoes in more ways than one.

That first day the party penetrated deep into the brushland pastures. Many times they encountered giant steers which lifted their heads and gazed at them aggressively. Men stood guard, their guns at the ready, the others getting to work. By nightfall, they had branded some thirty calves. Weary, they struck camp and slept beneath the stars. The following morning they breakfasted on beans, sowbelly and strong Arbuckle's coffee before recommencing their task.

It was at noon that day, with the heat risen, that they were startled by the alarmed mooing of a cow from deeper in the thicket. Hardeman signalled a halt and they drew up and dismounted. Leaving their mustangs, they moved forward through the tangled growth, encountering the familiar smell of singeing hide. A moment later they burst into a clearing and found five men grouped near a small fire and armed with a branding-iron, working on a wild calf. Its roped mother looked on.

Hardeman's arrival immediately spread consternation. This was clearly a party of maverickers, shaggy and filthy, and several of them instantly drew bandannas over their faces, but not before Hardeman had recognized the Gausman twins among them. The Gausmans ran a small-holding some ten miles south of Ballard's Valley. Both possessed the same high forehead with prominent brows and eyes deep-set in the skull. Both had ratnest beards, and cultivated their similarity by wearing identical clothing, each subsequently blaming the other if discovered up to no good. However on this day they had both been caught red-handed and there was no denying their criminal intent of branding illegally.

Both parties glared at each other in stunned silence. The Double-X men held their carbines but not in threatening fashion. The calf was released, rose on to its wobbly legs and scrambled across to its mother, its newly burned brand still smoking.

'Mavericking is illegal!' Seth Hardeman's voice came harshly.

'You got to prove it first,' Cal Gausman snarled, drawing his gun.

'Hold on,' his brother Cornelius shouted. 'Ain't no need for gunplay. Maybe we can talk things through.'

At that moment Billy Seymour, one of the Double-X cowhands, made a mistake by moving suddenly. Cal Gausman saw it as a threat and fired his gun, the bullet striking Seymour between the eyes, hurling him backwards in a splattering of blood. The action caused immediate mayhem as more guns were yanked from their holsters.

Men hurled themselves aside, the snap of gunfire burning their ears. Hardeman let out a grunt as a bullet ploughed into his chest, having him twisting away and down.

Frank Batty threw himself at Cal Gausman, catching him a vicious blow across the skull with the barrel of his carbine, dropping him like a felled ox. For a moment, the air seemed a haze of redness as lead and blood mingled with gunsmoke.

Somehow, within it all, Cornelius Gausman and his surviving maverickers melted back into the mesquite in scrambling retreat. Seth Hardeman lay stunned upon the ground, blood pumping from his chest. Frank Batty had his gun rammed against Cal Gausman's head as the latter struggled back to sensibility, blaspheming over and over. Bilson, Plommer and Sterner had all escaped injury and now they realized the futility of giving chase to the maverickers. This was the first time they had ever known Seth Hardeman to be out-foxed and it didn't rest easy with them. Had they gone in with carbines blazing, Billy Seymour might still be alive and Hardeman himself not be knocking at hell's door.

But at least they had somebody on whom to vent their anger — Cal Gausman.

'Let's lynch the skunk!' Ben Pommer shouted. 'He sure don't deserve nothin' better!' and Sterner was grunting agreement. He was, in fact, turning back towards his mustang for his rope. At that moment the crack of a pistol sounded, startling everybody. All eyes swung to Pommer. He had shot the calf in the head. It was common practice to leave the body of the calf which had been illegally branded beneath the dangling feet of the lynched man as a grim reminder to others who might consider breaking the law.

Seth Hardeman had somehow drawn himself up, was sitting slumped against the gnarled trunk of a tree, his chest sodden with blood, his breath a wheezing, faltering gasp. Vomit was trickling down the side of his jaw. Bilson had ripped aside his shirt to examine the wound and cursed at what he saw.

'Get some moss,' he snapped out. 'Be quick, for Gawd's sake. Maybe we can stem the bleeding a bit. We got to get him back to the ranch. He sure ain't gonna last long unless we get a doctor.'

As the others hesitated, he added: 'We'll take Gausman back, hand him over to the law in Kwahadi Springs. No time for a lynchin' now!'

Pommer started to argue but when he glanced at Hardeman, meeting his angry glare, he backed down. 'Let's get Gausman tied up then,' he conceded.

The journey back, roped to the back of his mustang to prevent him falling off, was white-hot agony for Seth Hardeman. Weakened by loss of blood, he lapsed in and out of delirium. More than once his men thought he had passed away, but then his laboured breathing would recommence and they pushed on through thicket and across streams, with Billy Seymour lying dead across his mount, and the bound Cal

Gausman stumbling along on foot at a rope's end, his deep-set eyes glinting with hatred as he cursed and spat at his captors.

2

That Texas morning Adam Ballard rode through the outbuildings of the Double-X ranch, greatly awed by the expansive lay-out compared with the sparse meandering of shacks that had once been his home. He only encountered one person who questioned his intrusion. A Mexican worker, a man with squat, bandy legs, a complete stranger, stepped out from the shadow of a barn and asked what he wanted.

Adam took a deep breath, then said: 'This is my home.'

The Mexican didn't respond, simply looked at him with puzzled eyes, perhaps having an inkling of his identity, but he made no attempt to bar his way.

Adam dismounted at the stoop of the fine house, hitched his bay horse to the rail, mounted the steps and walked into the cool interior of the main room. Its opulence nigh took his breath away, for there were richly coloured curtains and cushions and the room was lavishly furnished with a sofa, high-backed leather chairs and tables with ornate legs, all of which must have been brought from the East. Everything was spotlessly clean and tidy and there was a young Mexican girl at the far side, busy with a duster. She immediately paused in her work and looked at him.

'*Buenos dias, señor,*' she murmured.

'I am Adam Ballard,' he announced. 'I want to speak with my stepmother.'

He swore her dusky skin became paler. She gestured to a side door. 'In the kitchen, *señor*.' A tremor showed in her voice.

He walked past her and found his stepmother. She was busy at the kitchen table, kneading dough in a bowl, a smudge of flour on her cheek. A cauldron of tasty-smelling meat simmered gently on a huge black cook-stove and an impressive water-pump stood on a shelf. Hannah immediate raised her face and focused her obsidian eyes upon him — large, reproachful eyes that retained their old aloofness. Eyes that he'd prayed would one day show the faintest suggestion of softness, of compassion, but they never had.

No greeting warmed the dry line of her lips. 'I knew you'd come sooner or later and I dreaded this day. You are not welcome, Adam. You were always bad seed and I curse that your mother ever gave birth to you.'

He was taken aback. He hadn't expected to be welcomed with open arms, but the coldness of her manner cut him like a blade.

'I have no other place to go,' he said. 'This my home.'

She returned to kneading the dough, working with exaggerated industry.

'Where's Hardman?' he enquired. 'Does he still work for you?'

She was a small, slim woman, almost birdlike in movement. Yet there was an

18

underlying toughness to her. Her hair was brushed severely back from her face. She cleared her throat.

'Seth's still here, Adam. I am married to him. You killed your father, my husband. You left me with little option but to find another man. Seth's away at the moment, branding calves in the *brasada*. He's a good husband. I suggest you're gone by the time he gets back.'

'I never killed my father,' Adam said.

She shot him a withering glare. 'That's not what the judge thought. That's not what the jury thought. That's not what anybody thought. Maybe you've convinced yourself with your own lies.'

'I . . . ' He started to speak but he heard movement behind him. He turned and saw his sister Altha enter the kitchen.

The sight of her stunned him. He struggled to convince himself that it was actually her. Despite the severity of their parents, their childhood had been full of fun. Of similar build to her stepmother, slim with small breasts, her skin had blanched. Eight years had altered her beyond anything natural. Her once bronzed hair had gone completely white. She was skinny and pallid, with her big eyes completely over-shadowing the rest of her face, shining and reddened as if with endless weeping. The happy, bright child with rosy complexion and glistening, burnished hair he could remember was hardly recognizable as she strove with almost manic effort to welcome him.

Her manner contrasted starkly with that of her stepmother, for her expression brightened and she spoke his name and threw herself into his arms in an embrace, her lips moist against his cheek 'Adam . . . Adam. I've prayed to God you'd come home!'

He laughed, overcome by the sheer warmth of her welcome. He had brought a small present for her, a crimson silk shawl which he knew she would love, for she favoured shawls, wearing them to conceal the strawberry birthmark that marred the side of her neck. He had brought a present for his stepmother also, a pretty butterfly brooch, but she expressed no gratitude, leaving it untouched upon the table.

For a second time he turned to Altha, again taking her in his arms, happy beyond words that he had found a spark of warmth in his homecoming.

'We must get him something to eat, Ma,' Altha was saying. 'He must be starvin'.'

But before Hannah could show any response they all heard a commotion, a shouting of men's voices and pounding of hoofs from outside, and they rushed from the kitchen through the main room to the stoop at the front of the house. All eyes were immediately drawn to the bloodied frame of Seth Hardeman. He was slumped forward in his saddle, a makeshift bandage draped across his chest. He looked as if he had been through a meat-grinder.

'Oh dear God!' Hannah screamed,

her hands fluttering about her lips like butterflies.

Even as they stood, shocked by the sight, Frank Batty and Greg Sterner were swinging from their mounts, dragging the bound Cal Gausman forward.

'We'll take the wagon into town, hand Gausman over to the law. We'll get Doc Fischer back here just as soon as we can!'

Meanwhile Hannah rushed forward to help Jack Bilson lift Hardeman from his mount. His face was twisted with pain. His shirt was sodden with blood and he smelled of grease and smoke. He tried to speak but all he emitted was a gasp of pain.

Adam noticed the body lashed to the back of a mustang — a Double-X man who'd obviously paid the full penalty in the *brasada* gunfight.

Within minutes the buckboard wagon had left for town, bearing the venomous-looking prisoner, breathing curses into his rat-nest beard. In the main room of the house, Seth Hardeman had been rested down on a couch, bustled over by Hannah. He looked in a poorly state. How he had survived the journey back from the *brasada* was a miracle; many a lesser man would have succumbed, but he still had an element of strength left in him. He had his eyes open when Adam followed into the room. Somehow Hardeman focused his sulphurous stare on him and mouthed the words: 'Oh God. Him!' then he lapsed into the misery of his suffering.

Adam turned away, knowing any assistance he could give was not required. Instead, outside, he found the Mexican who had first greeted him, and together they untied Billy Seymour's corpse from the back of his mustang, laid it out in a barn and covered it with a blanket. Later, Adam found a sheltered meadow on the eastern side of the ranch where several other crosses marked burying places. The Mexican helped him dig a hole deep enough to take Seymour's remains. It would serve as a grave until, and if, his family subsequently claimed the body or wished to say prayers. He had not known the man, but, as they laid the body to rest, he felt a tinge of sadness that anybody of such youth should be cut short in life.

Afterwards, Adam attended to his own horse, slipping the saddle from its back, working with a brush he found, causing the animal a degree of ecstasy as he rubbed at worn patches. Afterwards, he set it to graze in the meadow.

He sat for a while in the shade of a nearby shed and contemplated what he was going to do. Clearly, apart from what came from Altha, there was no welcome for him here — yet he knew that if he was to stand any chance of proving his innocence he would have to base himself at the Double-X. But the eight-year-old trail had gone cold and where he should begin remained a problem. His mind kept hovering back to Hardeman. He knew that his father had had a few enemies, but on reflection it seemed that the person who had gained the most from his death had been Hardeman, inheriting not only the potential of the ranch — but also his wife.

He tried to put the thought aside, determined not to jump at any rash conclusions, but the feeling persisted.

Presently Altha joined him. Together they sat cross-legged on the earth as they had done so often as children, and she told him what she had learned from the men who had been with Hardeman when they had encountered the Gausman twins and their crew.

'Pity they didn't shoot 'em all down,' she said bitterly. 'They'll put Cal Gausman on trial. He'll get the rope for sure.'

Adam nodded. He couldn't take his eyes off his sister and the sight saddened him.

'Why's your hair gone white?' he asked bluntly.

She sighed heavily. 'I guess things just got too much for me. What with Pa

gettin' killed, you goin' to prison
. . . and then losin' Jimmy . . . ' She
stifled a sob at the mention of the
name.

'Jimmy?' he prompted.

'Jimmy Caldwell was a sweet boy. We
were goin' to be married, but he was
killed in the war. Shot down at Shiloh.'

Adam nodded. He had a vague
recollection of young Jimmy Caldwell.
He'd been a bright, easygoing lad with
chipmunk cheeks, but he'd never
realized that his sister had such strong
feelings for him.

'I'm sorry, Altha,' he said. 'I guess it
was a bad time for you. It was for us
all.'

She gave him a steady gaze. 'Had I
not had faith in the Lord,' she said. 'I
guess I'd have gone mad.'

An hour later the buckboard wagon
returned from Kwahadi Springs bringing the rotund doctor, Wilbur Fischer, a
veteran of the crude medical demands
of the area. He had bushy sideburns, a
double chin and thick, rimless glasses

which he polished frequently. He half-fell from the wagon and rushed into the house clutching his bag of medical supplies.

He was amazed that Seth Hardeman still survived, unleashing a scorching curse when he first saw the nature of the wound. Hardeman had lapsed into a coma. His loss of blood had been massive. Fischer rolled up his sleeves, ordered a bowl of boiling water, spread his instruments on the table and set to work showing little optimism. Meanwhile Hannah watched with distraught eyes.

The doctor administered a generous dose of opium and made a deep incision, concluding that the bullet had sliced between Hardeman's ribs, narrowly missing the aorta but nicking the gullet and then exiting through his back. He had vomited into his left chest cavity. There, on the kitchen table of the Double-X ranch, Doctor Fischer worked until late evening in his struggle to save this man's life, while Hannah held the kerosene lamp, and by the time he had finished and the patient lay heavily sedated, he gave no guarantee as to the chances of survival. If he did live, then he would require weeks of rest.

But by next morning, in the weakest of conditions, Hardeman was to rally and insist that his men returned to their task of branding calves before some other bastards got their irons on to them.

3

With dawn thinning the shadows of her room, Altha awoke that Sunday and suffered the usual bout of morning sickness which had plagued her this past week or so. She was deeply perplexed. For a moment she stood, her sad eyes closed, while tears ran down her pallid cheeks. After she had dressed and descended the stairs, she peered into the main room and saw how her stepfather remained on the couch, covered by a blanket, his breathing laboured but steady. Hannah sat over him, keeping a constant vigil, her head occasionally bobbing, from the weariness caused by the sleepless night.

Altha went for her customary walk in the glimmerings of the new day, wondering where Adam had bedded for the night. Like her brother's mind, hers was filled with joyful recollections of their childhood romps in this paradise of a valley, climbing trees, cavorting naked in streams, fishing with cane poles and homespun cotton string, riding the spirited mustangs and sometimes getting thrown. But now that all seemed a hundred years ago. She wondered if her stepmother would ever soften her heart towards Adam. Presently she returned to her room and sat reading the Bible for an hour.

At nine o'clock she walked to the bunkhouse where Joe Lanum awaited with a big mare between the shafts of a fringe-top wagon ready to take her to church in Kwahadi Springs, a journey of some ten miles. This was his unfailing Sunday duty. He was a good-natured man, though unfortunately afflicted by a bad stammer which made communication difficult. Within ten minutes they were on the trail. It was deeply pot-holed and bumpy but she suffered the discomfort without complaint.

They had travelled six miles and

rounded a bend in the trail following the curve of the river, when they were confronted by a rope strung across infront of them. Lanum hauled on the reins bringing the wagon to a halt, stammering a curse, but he was given no time to contemplate, for a skinny man with a rat-nest beard stepped from behind a boulder — Cornelius Gausman. His revolver was levelled at Lanum.

'Get off the wagon!' he demanded.

Lanum hesitated but Gausman gestured with his gun menacingly, and his deep-set eyes showed a wildness that brooked no argument. Lanum slid from his seat, dropped on to the trail. Meanwhile Altha watched from the wagon helplessly.

Keeping his gun aimed at Lanum, Gausman leaped on to the wagon-seat with considerable agility for his fifty years, then he tossed a paper down at Lanum's feet.

'Deliver that to the Double-X,' he growled. 'Make sure they understand

31

what it says! Get walking and don't you look back.'

He jerked on the reins and set the horse forward at a pace that rapidly grew to a gallop.

Lanum drew his gun, sent a bullet winging after the departing wagon. He cursed. His weapon was no more accurate than a pea-shooter and anyway he dare not fire too close for fear of hitting the girl. He stood with the paper in one hand, the smoking gun in the other, watching the dust gradually settling, hearing the rattle of the wagon grow fainter in the distance. Anger flared in him. He slammed his gun into its holster, removed his hat, flung it on the ground and stamped on it. He didn't care to be out-smarted by that old scoundrel, but everything had come so unexpected.

He glanced at the paper. Words were scrawled on it:

Unless Cal Gausman is released immediately, the girl dies. That's a promise!

After a moment Lanum retrieved his hat, rammed it on his head and started his bandy-legged stomp back towards the ranch.

★ ★ ★

It was a hard slog in the blistering heat to the ranch. He stumbled through the outbuildings, encountering nobody, for most of the men had obeyed the ailing Hardeman's gasped orders and returned to the *brasada* with their branding-irons. Adam Ballard was the first to meet Lanum. Anxious to make himself useful, he'd been cleaning out a hog-pen when he saw the distressed cowboy appear. Now he extracted from him the stammered news.

'C-Cornelius G-Gausman. He ambushed the w-wagon. He's kidnapped Altha. Look!' He held out the sweat-stained paper. Adam scanned the words and groaned in anguish.

'Damn the man!' He rushed towards the house. His stepmother would have to be informed. He found her in the kitchen, preparing some gruel for her patient. She glared at him, then took the note, her eyes gradually widening.

'Oh my God!' she groaned, passing a hand across her careworn brow. 'What can we do?' Adam realized she was looking at him with panic rising in her face. 'Adam . . . what can we do?'

He realized that in this moment her hatred had been forgotten. He was the only one she could turn to.

'I'll ride along the trail,' he said, 'see if I can find any trace. If not, I'll go straight in Kwahadi Springs and inform the law.'

'Do you think they'll let Gausman go?' she asked in a desperate voice. 'If they don't I'm sure Cornelius will do somethin' bad to Altha. He's a real wicked man.'

Adam shook his head. 'I'll try my best. Maybe I can pick up his trail.'

She reached out, gripping his arm, touching him for the first time since his return. 'Adam, be careful!'

He nodded and turned towards the door, not knowing whether her concern was for himself or on Altha's account. There was no time to find out.

He saddled his horse, checked his weapons and rode out. It was years since he had followed the trail to town, but it was a lonely way that had changed little. Lanum had spoken of the spot where the river curved. That must be his first point of investigation.

The sun was a scorching ball above him as he rode. He paused only occasionally to rest the bay horse. He followed the wagon-tracks easily enough and covered the six miles to the river bend without mishap; nonetheless, apprehension was burning inside him. He'd never heard of the Gausman twins before, but already he was forming a picture of evil and unscrupulous men and the prospect of Altha being at Cornelius's mercy had him grinding his teeth with misery. His sole intent on release from prison had been to establish the truth behind the injustice which he had suffered, but now events had overtaken him and Altha's fate had assumed the first priority.

Sure enough, he found where the wagon had skewed to a halt, and there were footprints in the dust revealing the activity which had occurred. He glanced around at the surrounding boulder-strewn slopes. It would have been the easiest place in the world to stage an ambush. Following the wheel-ruts, he travelled a good mile down the trail before the tracks veered off to the side. He was aware that a hidden marksman could easily take a shot at him, but he consoled himself with the thought that Cornelius was hardly likely to have lingered in this vicinity any longer than necessary. Now he searched the area and found the wagon, complete with horse still standing in the shafts in a clump of trees. He dismounted, scouted around and shortly found where two horses had been left tethered. These were now departed, leaving no tracks across the rocky slope, and he was convinced that Gausman and Altha were long gone. God only knew where Gausman had taken her, but it was sure to be somewhere not easily traced.

He decided to travel on to town and report matters to the marshal.

He hitched his own horse to the tail of the wagon, climbed on to the seat and drove onward.

Kwahadi Springs had spread out since his last visit and many of the false-front buildings had given way to solid structures. The wide street was now lined with stores, today closed for the Sabbath, and there was a saloon, a bank, a café, a funeral parlour, a telegraph office, a trading and livery barn — and of course the church where Altha should have worshipped that morning. He soon found the town marshal's office, and to his satisfaction the door stood open. He drew up the wagon, dismounted and climbed on to the sidewalk, noting the board that proclaimed: *Amos McCrain, Town Marshal Kwahadi Springs*. He entered the office, the walls of which were plastered with reward dodgers, to be greeted by the deep-chested cough of a clearly sick man.

Amos McCrain had been slumped forward over his desk but now he straightened up, drawing the back of his hand across his mouth. Adam had never met him previously.

'My God,' McCrain wheezed. 'I sure do feel bad.'

Adam was too stirred up with the purpose of his mission to express sympathy. 'My name's Adam Ballard from the Double-X. My sister's been kidnapped by Cornelius Gausman. He's threatening to kill her unless his brother's released.' He handed McCrain the note which he read.

'Well, I'll be doggone!' McCrain said. 'Always knew them Gausman twins were trash.'

The marshal's fingers showed a tremble. He'd once been a handsome man, with a waterfall moustache, had built up a fine reputation over past years and maintained peace in Kwahadi

38

Springs since coming to office. But now he was a sorry sight with hollowed eye-sockets and a stoop to his shoulders. He coughed again as he returned the note.

'Where's Cal Gausman now?' Adam asked, conscious that every second they dallied increased the danger to his sister.

'In the town jail at the end of the street. No chance of him getting out of there. The mayor's payin' for a four-man guard, night and day.'

'Maybe we have to give in to Cornelius's threat,' Adam suggested, though the thought grieved him. 'My sister's life is at stake.'

McCrain gave his head a slow shake. 'The wheels 've been set in motion. I telegraphed the county sheriff and the circuit judge as soon as Cal Gausman was brought in. The judge is coming here next week. He don't waste much time, and nothing'll deter him from administerin' the law. I'm downright sorry about this. I'll sure do what I can to investigate the kidnappin'.'

Adam knew that the marshal's heart was in the right place, but his health was bad and that didn't bode well.

'He could have taken her anywhere,' McCrain remarked, rubbing his jaw.

'Where've the Gausmans got their homestead?' Adam enquired. 'I doubt he's holding her there — too obvious. But it's somewhere to start. Could be some clue there.'

'North side of town,' McCrain said. 'Follow the river along for five miles, then cut east at Pinnacle Rock. You can't mistake it. The cabin's a pretty wretched place, built in the lee of the hill.'

'Thanks.' Adam turned on his heel and minutes later was heading north out of town, his impatience having him pushing the bay horse hard.

He found the Gausman homestead. True enough, it had a derelict air about it. The cabin was surrounded by a number of sheds and about them hung the familiar smell that indicated they had been used for hide-tanning and the extraction of tallow. He dismounted in the yard, glanced around uneasily. He wondered if he was under surveillance. Was somebody gazing at him through the sights of a rifle? He shrugged the feeling off, stepped up on to the cabin's stoop, his hand hovering above the butt of his sawn-off .44.

He rapped his knuckles against the hewn door without response. He tried the door. It was secured. He stepped to the side and peered between tattered curtains through dirt-grimed windows. The interior appeared dark, but not dark enough to conceal the mess that littered the main room. He sighed heavily, pretty certain that nobody was around, then he made up his mind. Now was no time for half-measures. He returned to the door and rammed the sole of his foot against it with all his might, bringing a complaining creak from the old timbers. At the third attempt the lock burst inward, the door swung open and he stepped through.

The place stank of stale food that came from the stack of unwashed plates on the shelf. Flies entered the room, buzzed about whatever scraps they could find. Papers were littered over the earthen floor. There were two bedrooms, each in the same mess as the main room, the unmade beds — simply boards nailed together into a frame, a heap of soiled blankets and ticks piled on them, an unemptied chamber-pot adding a pungent odour to the atmosphere.

Adam cursed and returned his attention to the main room. A sudden sound from outside caused him to stiffen; his hand closed over the butt of his gun, then he realized it was only his horse pawing the ground impatiently. He forced himself to relax, but despair was deepening in him. He doubted he would find any clue to Altha's whereabouts in this place. The two brothers had obviously been living here alone. He should have realized that Cornelius would be too crafty to bring his prisoner to his home.

As he turned towards the door, his gaze fell upon an old desk standing against the wall. He stepped across to it, tried to open the drawer but it was locked. This roused his curiosity. He drew his gun, then hesitated. A shot would attract the attention of anybody in the vicinity, but impatience got the better of him. He placed the muzzle against the drawer and pressed the trigger. The blast filled the room, brought a ringing to his ears — but the drawer was splintered open. Inside he found a collection of papers. With the smell of gunsmoke in his nostrils, he shuffled through them. They were mainly bills of sale for hides, then he found a thick wad of green-back banknotes. Last of all he noticed a letter, scrawled in an untidy hand. It was undated but it was heavily creased and he guessed it had been in the drawer for some time.

Dear Cornelius

I am sorry to say I am leaving you. I cannot live with your illegal ways any longer, not knowing when the law will come for you and Cal. I am going to stay with my sister until I can find somewhere more permanent.

Your wife
Irma

Adam sighed. He collected the bills of sale, money and letter, bundled them together and stuffed them in his pockets. He would hand them over to the law in Kwahadi Springs, what there was of it! But at least this could prove useful evidence for the judge when he arrived next week.

Feeling sure he would find nothing else of value in this place, he left.

4

He had returned to town by mid-afternoon. A feeling of helplessness was growing in him. God knew what Gausman was doing with his sister. He fully expected that Gausman would keep his word: if anything happened to Cal, his brother would murder Altha — and there was little doubt that a guilty verdict would be reached and that would mean a hanging.

Intent on handing over the items of possible evidence, he went to the marshal's office but found it closed. The keeper of a close-by hardware store paused as he swept his frontage and informed Adam that the marshal had gone home feeling sick. He explained where McCrain's house was, on the edge of town. He lived with his daughter Kathleen.

Adam had no desire to hang on to

the money in case he was accused of theft. The sooner he handed it over and got a receipt the better, so he found the marshal's home, hitched his mount to the gate, walked up a path through a pretty flower garden where a chinaberry tree grew, stepped up on to the long front veranda and knocked at the door. It was opened by a young woman who he guessed must be McCrain's daughter. She was slender and youthful. Her sweetly expressive face was full of concern as she looked at him enquiringly.

'I'm Adam Ballard,' he said. 'My sister's been kidnapped . . . '

'Oh yes. Daddy told me you called. I'm terribly sorry . . . ' Her voice had a huskiness about it that he found attractive.

'I've got some things I wanted to hand over to your father, some evidence that may prove useful at Cal Gausman's trial.'

She glanced back over her shoulder, a look of harassment clouding her face.

'It's strange,' she said. 'Daddy didn't seem too bad when he first came home, but then he said he wanted to lie down and that's when he took a bad turn. I'm really worried about him. I had to fetch Doctor Fischer. He's with him now.'

He was taken aback. 'I'm sorry. If anybody can help him, I'm sure Wilbur Fischer will. He's a real good doctor. Anyway, I mustn't keep you. I'm sure you've got a lot to attend to. I do hope your dad feels better soon. I'll be on my way . . . '

'Oh no. Come in for a moment,' she insisted. 'I'll take those things off you. Lock them up safe.'

He hesitated but her insistence had him stepping into the neat parlour decorated with ornaments, bookshelves and scenic pictures. It was a house with strong walls and many-paned windows that attracted the sun and seemed in stark contrast to much of the town where men brawled and drunkards lolled. He could hear Doctor Fischer's voice coming from the adjoining room.

He sounded awful serious.

'Put the stuff on the table,' she said. 'I'll make sure it's stored somewhere safe and when the judge arrives I'll hand it over to him.'

'There's some money,' he said. He watched her as she took the bundle of notes and, showing sudden efficiency, quickly counted it — $640. She wrote out a receipt and gave it to him, then she glanced at Irma Gausman's letter.

'Gone to live with her sister,' she murmured. She scratched her chin thoughtfully. 'She lives in Waco. I remember Irma once told me.'

At that moment Doctor Fischer called from the next room and Kathleen turned and rushed in. Adam followed her, stood in the doorway of the room — obviously Amos's bedroom. He was lying very still beneath a patchwork quilt, his face looking a ghastly grey despite his tan.

Fischer's rotund face was creased with gravity. 'He's had a seizure, my dear. He's very ill. I can't do much more for him . . . '

'Is he dying?' Kathleen enquired in a querulous voice.

Fischer didn't answer directly. 'He's lapsed into a coma. I can't guarantee he'll come round.'

'Oh God,' Kathleen sobbed. 'What can I do?'

'Pray, my dear,' Fischer consoled. 'Only the Lord can save him.' He reached out, put his arm around the distraught girl. 'He's been a wonderful lawman in his time. Kwahadi Springs owes him a lot.'

A surge of compassion passed through Adam. He felt immensely sad for this girl. She obviously loved her father dearly, He felt a desperate urge to back out, to leave Kathleen to her private grief, yet somehow he seemed rooted to the spot. He wished he had some way to comfort her.

In fact within the next hour he did provide help. He went for the under-taker because the town marshal had passed away, and after the body had been removed to the funeral parlour and the doctor had expressed his heartfelt sorrow and departed, Kathleen wept in his arms and he smoothed her raven hair with a gentle hand and made soothing sounds — and he thought how strange it was. He'd known her only a few hours, had never dreamed when he had come to the house that he would hold this girl, feel her body soft and yielding against his own. She came to him without any self-consciousness, as if he'd been her brother and despite the sadness of the moment, a fleeting happiness touched him, made him temporarily forget his own troubles.

★　★　★

During the following days the urgency increased in him, the sense that time for Altha was running out and that the real moment of truth for her would come when Judge Edgar Ramsburg delivered his verdict. His feelings for Altha had deepened during her absence. His mind was filled with recollections of the childhood they had spent together. As siblings there had been no rivalry between them, just a bond forged by a firm-handed parentage in which they both shared a desire to kick over the traces. But the thought of Altha as she was now, a ghost of her old self, haunted him. She had taken the knocks of life truly hard, and he felt there was something almost unhealthy in the way in which she pinned her life and hopes to faith in the Lord. Not that he had anything against the Lord, but He had his place, same as everybody else — God provided a path in life and it was up to a person to plot a way through.

But, more than anything else now, he wanted to get Altha back and try to restore in her some vestige of happiness.

He bedded down and fed in the bunkhouse at the Double-X. Each morning he was astride a spirited mustang and riding into the *brasada*. It was quite possible that Cornelius Gausman had some hideaway deep in the thickets where he was holding Altha. Trying to find it in brushland over a hundred miles wide was a formidable task, yet the determination was in him to try.

Full of dark, sinister places the *brasada* might be, but Adam was not blind to its beauty. Amid the thorn mesquite, Texas ironwood, and chaparral, where multicoloured blooms such as jasmine, retama and grey cinizo which burst into wondrous lavender bloom after rain. And the thickets and meadows not only teemed with feral bovines, but with herds of white-collared pigs, *javelinas*, which rooted out the yucca bulbs. There were also armadillos, kangaroo-rats and countless types of snakes.

However Adam's mind was not dwelling on Nature's beauty but on the prospect of picking up some trail or sign that would indicate that other humans had passed this way. He rode, spooking bunches of wild steers. But once he was almost caught off guard. A macho steer, a yellow *ladino*, enraged by his intrusion, charged out of the undergrowth like a cannon-ball — a ton of bone and muscle. In mid-leap he slammed his left horn at the flank of Adam's mustang, but Adam jerked his mount to the side, avoiding disaster by a fraction. The horn of the wild beast ripped Adam's chaps before it charged on and was gone from sight, crashing through the solid wall of the thicket, leaving man and mount shaken and starkly reminded of the dangers that lurked in the *brasada*.

Even so, he carried on his search, trying to fend off the feeling that it was a futile endeavour. He was angry that each passing minute brought Altha closer to a terrible fate.

It was usually nightfall before he returned to the Double-X. His step-mother always greeted him with her customary coldness, expecting little from his efforts to find Altha. After a few days, Seth Hardeman was sitting up on his bed, swathed in bandages, his rugged face reflecting pain and frustration. He was still having trouble keeping food down and breathing. It would be a good time before he was strong enough to place his feet upon the ground, let alone to mount a horse and ride out. He would listen, grunting sourly, as Adam related how he'd searched the *brasada*.

'You'll never find that girl out there,' he said. 'At least not before Gausman has killed her, because it is a sure thing his brother will swing.'

'Don't talk like that, Seth,' Hannah reproved. 'Cornelius may not be as mean as he makes out.'

Hardeman shook his head. 'We shall see. The trial's tomorrow. I've written out a statement. It'll be read out in court.'

'What you said may affect Altha's life,' Adam said. 'You gave evidence once before. Remember?'

'I told the truth, that's all, both then and now. Justice was done then and will be now.'

Adam met Hardeman's long withering stare and did not flinch. Was he gazing into the eyes of the man who had killed his father?

His stepmother broke the spell, her voice cutting through the tension that lay between the two men.

'You must carry on searching, Adam. You've got to find her before that awful man does his worst. Poor Altha. Find her, Adam. That's the least you can do for this family.'

Adam tore his gaze away from Hardeman's dark eyes.

Each day would find him back in the *brasada*, combing ever deeper, searching the banks of streams and soft places for hoofprints that were not cloven.

He found the spot where the gunfight had taken place, indicated by spent shell cases and the dark marks of blood that still showed upon the ground. He also found the decomposed remains of a calf, ravaged by nature and scavengers. It was lying at the foot of a mesquite tree which so easily could have been used as a lynching tree. Strangely, part of the hide had been preserved and this clearly bore the illegal brand which the maverickers had placed on it: the simple outline of a rocking chair.

He circled wider and wider, desperate for sign. Sure enough he found tracks, but these were of the horsemen who had fled from the scene of the fight, and were now stale with grass and insect life renewed in the depressions, and were thus of little use.

He carried on searching, gradually despairing and daunted by the vastness of the land. But one evening, when he stopped at a streamside to refresh his horse and take a bite to eat, he was far closer to Cornelius Gausman than even his wildest dreams would have foretold. For a whole minute his head was squarely within the sights of Gausman's rifle, the rat-nest-bearded man's trigger finger curled restlessly within the trigger-guard.

Gausman lay pressed against the ground, hidden in the shadow of the mesquite. He debated whether or not to kill Adam Ballard now, for he had no doubt as to his identity. But then it occurred to him, that unlike his brother, he was not yet guilty of murder. Mavericking was a hanging offence, but it had to be proved and some judges were more lenient than others. In consequence, he rested his gun down and allowed Adam to proceed on his way.

He waited until sound of Adam's departure had long died into the distance, then remained another twenty minutes before rising from his hiding-place and back-tracking the two miles to where the girl was held.

Ballard was getting too close in his searching and Gausman would have to move on shortly. But he was aware that tomorrow was the day of Cal's trial in Kwahadi Springs and he had arranged for one of his cohorts, Sam Pitts, to bring word of the outcome to him. The girl's fate would depend on that outcome. He owed Pitts money from their last sale of hides and when a man was due payment he tended to be reliable, so Cornelius had little doubt that as soon as the judge made his pronouncement, Sam Pitts would carry word. He was one of the few who knew where Gausman had his hideaway. It would be hell to find, in the deepest thicket, for anybody uninformed.

An hour later he was back at the hideaway — a hovel hollowed out in the mesquite, thatched heavy with thorny boughs. Inside he could build a hatful of fire without fear of the smoke carrying.

It was here that Altha Ballard was held prisoner, bound hand and foot, lashed to a tree to prevent her from crawling off. The journey here had been tortuous, one which she had experienced with dismay. She had watched with increasing unease as they had progressed into a wilderness so immense, so remotely uninhabited, that it dwarfed any she had previously thought of as wild. She was pale and weak, but she remained sullen and silent, her eyes deep pools of resentment. At night she lay tense and sleepless, listening to the shrill yapping of coyotes and once she heard the coughing challenge of a cougar. Several times, during daylight, she saw tarantulas, the size of supper-plates, scuttling over the ground, and rattlesnakes sunning themselves on rocks.

He had tried to be sociable, tried to draw her into conversation, but the only word she ever spoke was when she wanted to relieve herself, and then he would lead her off, like a hound on a halter, and waited impatiently until she was finished.

There were times when the thought of having a woman completely at his mercy created a tingle of excitement in him. It was years since he'd had a real woman. Irma had dried up on him years ago — and she was long gone now anyway. Now he looked at Altha, seeing her small breasts thrusting against her tattered dress. He wondered what her body was like stripped naked. He swallowed hard. He'd cared for this bitch well enough, he'd fed her. She'd had her share of the pig-meat he'd taken.

He moved across towards her. She cringed back from him, but her eyes showed defiance.

'Maybe it's time you was a little bit friendly to old Cornelius,' he said.

She noticed how the drippings from countless meals lay clotted within the dark tangle of his beard.

'My old woman was as mean as a polecat, but I bet you'll be real sweet.'

He heard saliva shunt back in her mouth.

'Don't you spit at me,' he said, his hand latching on to her skirt, ripping it up over her pale thighs.

She spat, leaving saliva drooling through the hairs on his cheeks. He cursed her and went crazy.

60

5

That day Judge Edgar Ramsburg of the Federal District and Circuit Court had arrived in town and been accommodated in *The Kwahadi Springs Hotel*, where, after a hearty meal, he'd settled down to studying his notes and the other evidence. He was an owlish-faced man from Massachusetts with a swallowtailed beard and intimidating eyes that glinted fiercely. He always wore a fine black broadcloth coat.

The two-storey town hall, a dreary grey stone building surrounded by a picket fence, had been especially prepared and there was a large attendance as indicated by the multitude of tied horses, wagons and buggies left outside. The selection of the jury had been a long process. With the clock on the towering cupola at the street's end pointing to nine, the prosecuting

61

attorney and the defending lawyer entered the grey stone courtroom. The prisoner was then brought from the town prison, his bearded face as bleak as a snowcapped mountain.

Adam stood on the sidewalk and watched the prisoner led across the street in chains. He saw little to be gained by attending the trial. He knew that one of the Double-X cowhands, Frank Batty, who had captured Cal Gausman in the first place, would be giving oral evidence. And of course there would be Seth Hardeman's written testimony. He doubted whether the fact that Altha had been kidnapped by the accused's brother would in anyway sway the judge. His owlish eyes would be focused purely on the administering of justice.

Determined to leave legal duties to those responsible, Adam turned towards his horse. He wondered how Kathleen McCrain was making out. He felt sorry for her and wished he could help her in some way — but he sensed she was a competent, strong woman who would learn to cope without her father. As he rode down the street he glanced along the sidewalks for sight of her, but she was not there. He hoped he would be able to see her again soon.

It occurred to him that either Cornelius Gausman or one of his sidekicks might visit his shack of a cabin to retrieve the money that had been left in the desk. They would have a shock when they discovered it was gone.

He felt that riding into the *brasada* again would be unproductive — and he knew now that matters were reaching a climax. By the end of the day, Judge Ramsburg might well have reached his verdict and issued sentence. The thought made him groan. Poor Altha. She'd been caught in the middle of this and never deserved such a fate.

Running out of ideas of where to search, he decided to head for the Gausman cabin. Maybe, just maybe, he might find some clue.

Whilst Adam was out of town, the trial got under way. Cal Gausman, looking drawn and evil, was formally charged with the murder of Billy Seymour. He pleaded not guilty, that he had acted in self-defence. The defence attorney, especially brought in from the county seat, acted on his behalf. But the prosecution stood firm, the statement of Seth Hardeman was read out and Frank Batty gave his eye-witness account of events. Furthermore, the large sum of cash that Adam had found at the Gausman homestead was considered to be ill-gotten, the fruit of criminal activity. All the evidence was totally damning, even down to Irma Gausman's letter in which she referred to her husband's illegal activity, the same sentiment clearly also applying to her brother-in-law. Judge Ramsburg, sitting in his straight-backed oak chair, speaking in his crisp Massachusetts nasality, was in a belligerent mood. The second charge, that of 'mavericking', simply rubbed salt into the wound. Texas law was simple and ruthless.

The jury pondered only briefly; their verdict was handed up, and the judge had delivered the sentence by mid-afternoon, glaring out from beneath his eyebrows, speaking in a doom-laden tone: 'Cal Gausman, you have had a fair trial and you have been found guilty on both charges. There is but one sentence to be passed down, and that is that, at a time decided by the local authority, you be hanged by the neck until you are dead. Under Texas law, you have no right of appeal. This session is now closed.' And he banged his gavel with a final flourish. The ashen-faced prisoner was frog-marched back to the town jail.

Before evening had set in, the judge had left town and carpenters were at work in the square erecting a gallows made from fresh-hewn pine, an ugly contraption, its macabre beam fourteen feet high. After execution the body would dangle twelve inches off the ground under the trap. Sentence was scheduled for three days hence.

Meanwhile, to his frustration, Adam found that nothing had changed at the Gausman homestead. There was no indication that anybody had visited the place since he had last been there.

★ ★ ★

The following day, Town Marshal Amos McCrain was buried in the fenced cemetery at the eastern edge of town. A considerable crowd gathered to see him laid to rest and pay their last respects. He had been a much esteemed lawman who had kept the peace in Kwahadi Springs for the last six years, having earned equal respect in his previous appointments. Adam stood next to Kathleen McCrain, admiring the fortitude which she showed. To his surprise and pleasure, he felt her arm slip through his after the minister had spoken his words, the earth was

66

shovelled in, and the final hymn was sung. 'We Shall Gather at the River'.

Although pale, she looked pretty in her black dress and dark, velvet bonnet trimmed with lace. She invited him back to her home for the simple gathering that followed the funeral and he accepted. He was becoming increasingly aware that he enjoyed her company — even in this moment when tears glistened in her eyes. She seemed to have no close relatives or other friends to whom she could turn.

But presently his pleasure was cut short by thoughts of his sister and the ordeal that she was suffering at this very moment — if, in fact, she still survived.

Harassed by his apprehensions, he left the gathering somewhat prematurely, but Kathleen, although grieving herself, showed great concern for the predicament he faced, and she saw him to the door, giving him a warm kiss on the cheek.

'Hope I can see you again soon, Adam,' she murmured, her eyes full of affection for him. 'But be careful. So many bad things are going on.'

He nodded, took her hand in both of his and gave it an appreciative squeeze, then he turned and left her.

As he rode down the street he crossed the town square and saw that the grim structure of the gallows was almost completed and the carpenters were standing back to admire their work with satisfied faces. He glanced up at the platform, saw the lever that would have it collapsing beneath the condemned man's feet, dropping him into oblivion — and shuddered. The hanging was scheduled for nine o'clock the next morning and he had heard that the newly appointed county hangman, George McCaffey, was due to arrive this evening, bringing his own ropes with him. Once Cal Gausman had gone to his maker, his brother would have no reason to keep Altha alive.

The rest of the day dragged intolerably. The sun blazed down with uncaring ferocity, baking everywhere into drowsy inactivity. The mayor had funded the heavy guard surrounding the blockhouse that was the town's jail, all heavily armed, and there was no sound from inside where Cal Gausman waited out his final hours. In the evening, the local minister, carrying his Bible, visited the prisoner, even reading passages to him, but Cal Gausman had never been a religious man and the fact that he was on the threshold of eternity brought no change in him. He was angry and embittered and whoever crossed his path was likely to feel his wrath.

Adam returned to the *brasada* still desperately hopeful that he might find some evidence of Cornelius's and Altha's presence, but he held out little hope. Here in the Big Thicket, a man could die alone and a hundred years might pass before another human stumbled across his bones. As the day waned and darkness settled over the brushland his heart was in his boots. For a while the temptation was in him to ride into town and disrupt the hanging party on the morrow, to maybe rescue Cal from the rope, but he soon realized how crazy such action would be.

He camped rough in the *brasada* that night, his horse hobbled and grazing on rich meadow grass. He rested his head on his saddle and watched the stars brighten the heavens, listening to the night sounds of the wilderness, particularly the lonesome sound of a loafer wolf mourning down the moon far out across the Trinity. He wondered if Altha could hear the same cry, sensed it as a premonition of the fate that awaited her.

He tried to make some sense out of past events. He had always loved his sister, even his father, who had endeavoured to instil discipline into him. But it was a hard task because Adam knew he had been a headstrong and irreverent boy, unruly as a yearling colt, and he had no doubt strained his father's patience to the extreme and thoroughly deserved the tongue lashings and beatings he'd received. But eight years in prison had given him ample time to think, had changed him, and he only wished he could somehow have brought his father back and made amends.

He had done his utmost to find Altha and would continue to do so until he had determined what had happened to her, one way or the other.

Next morning there was early activity In Kwahadi Springs as the hangman George McCaffey prepared his rope, rubbing oil into the fibres by hand, and inspected the gallows. This was his first official hanging and his nervousness must almost have equalled that of the condemned man. His fee was a hundred dollars out of which he had to buy a suit of clothes for the condemned man and a blanket and a pine coffin.

Only a small gathering of the most ghoulish had assembled to witness the execution. The majority of townsfolk stayed behind closed doors, curtains drawn, and had little stomach for this aspect of the due process of law — not that either of the Gausman twins had ever attracted much friendship, for they had always been viewed as sly, untrustworthy characters who kept to themselves.

As the town clock high on its handsome copula struck a solemn nine times, the shackled Cal Gausman was led from the town jail, surrounded by a posse of guards who had no intention of allowing any last-minute attempt to save their prisoner from his just deserts. His beard had been shaved off, giving him a much younger appearance. He was led up the sturdily made steps to the platform, the minister intoned a few meaningless words from the Holy Book, then a black hood was slipped over Gausman's head, followed by the virgin noose which the hangman checked for a good fit with apparent care.

But his care was insufficient, for Cal Gausman did not sustain the quick snap of the neck and instant death that all condemned men pray for. Instead, he took some fifteen minutes to die in choking, gagging and kicking agony that brought no credit to his executioner and made McCaffrey swear to do better next time.

* * *

Sam Pitts, a bull-necked man who had been in the Gausman party on that fateful day of the gunfight with the Double-X cowhands and had concealed his identity with a hastily drawn-up bandanna, had watched the grisly spectacle from the shadows of Jim's Tonsorial Parlour opposite, his bowels made tremulous by his knowledge of 'there but for the grace of God, go I . . .'

Now, having resigned himself to the fact that all was finished and that nothing short of heavenly intervention was going to bring Cal Gausman back to this world, he went for his horse hitched outside The Golden Nugget, left town and an hour later was riding hard into the *brasada*. The image of Gausman's final, horrific minutes of life haunted him like the worst nightmare, but he had promised to carry word to Cornelius and Cornelius was not one to cross. The brushland was strangely silent as he rode, apart from once when a covey of bobwhite quail burst skywards from the thicket, the flap of their wings coming with the sharpness of a gunshot, briefly scaring the wits out of him. When he eventually quit the narrow draw at the point where a lightning-struck mesquite tree stood, its blackened, downhanging branch some-how resembling a bird with a broken wing, he knew he was close to the hideaway.

He reined in his sweating mount, cupped his hands to his lips and emitted the shrill call of a curlew — three times in quick succession. Within a half-minute the response came and he heeled his animal forward knowing that he would not be greeted by a bullet.

Soon, he was seated close to the ramshackle hideaway, roasting pig on a stick over the fire and sipping Arbuckle's, relating his news to the grim-faced Cornelius. From within the shadows of the hideaway, he could see the pale girl, her hands and feet bound, watching them with her large sullen eyes.

Pitts was in no mood to spare Cornelius the gruesome facts of what he had witnessed.

'It was hell watching Cal choke to death with his hands fastened behind his back. He fought that rope like crazy, his tongue lolling . . . ' He couldn't go on. He dipped his head, closing his eyes, clicking his own tongue at the hideous image in his mind. 'That damned hangman deserves hanging hisself.'

Cornelius was trembling. 'Oh God . . . oh God.' He plunged his gaunt face into his hands, sobbing like a baby; then slowly he composed himself and the anger settled over him, giving him renewed strength, and he said, 'Somebody will pay for this . . . by hell I swear it!'

'Will you kill the girl?' Pitts asked.

Cornelius took a deep, tremulous breath. 'I'll do it. I said I'd do it and I will!'

Pitts didn't respond. He pulled at the pig-meat with yellow teeth, then he stood up. He would not linger here. He had no wish to be implicated in any murder that took place. He had enough sin on his conscience already.

'What'll you do afterwards?' he asked.

'I shall disappear,' Cornelius said. 'I'm finished here.'

Pitts didn't press him further. He nodded, said, 'Thanks for the victuals,' and moved into the mesquite to where his horse waited. He would be nigh home by nightfall. No lawman, right now, had anything on him.

Cornelius leaned back against a tree-trunk. He felt tired and sick.

Thoughts of Cal kept plaguing him. He closed his eyes, but the image would not leave him despite the fact that he fell into sleep. He did not know how long he remained so, but he did know that he awoke with a shout, the coarse feel of a rope about his neck. He was trying desperately to reach up and claw it away from his throat but his hands were fastened behind his back — and suddenly he couldn't swallow, could no longer shout and he was choking, choking.

Damn dream!

He shook his head to clear his senses. He was angry, furious. He heard a whimper come from the girl in the hideaway. He had said somebody would pay. It would be her; she deserved nothing better; she hadn't even obliged him when he'd offered her the chance of intimacy. She was polecat mean. He was trembling again, violently, as he drew his pistol from its holster and checked that there were rounds in the chamber. No different from killing a pig! he thought.

She watched him as he stumbled towards her, still dazed by the nightmare which had haunted him.

She watched him with her big cold eyes, crouching back against the lean-to. 'They killed my brother!' he snarled.

She met his insane eyes. Spittle glistened in his filthy beard. He raised the gun, his finger curled about the trigger.

'Do it!' she said.

At that moment he was not seeing her; he was seeing Cal choking and gagging away his life.

6

Next day Adam struck lucky, at least he thought he had, for he cut the hoof-marks of Sam Pitts's horse and followed them up the draw. He was close to the lightning-struck mesquite tree when he heard a strange, insistent scraping sound. He reined in, nerves tense, senses straining for an explanation. Still puzzled, he slipped from his saddle, drew his gun and crept towards the sound. A minute later he discovered a big wolf. As soon as the animal saw him it was off, loping away into the shadowy thicket.

Adam moved forward and saw that the wolf had been scratching at a freshly turned patch of earth. A sinking feeling hit his stomach. He glanced around to make sure he was unobserved — and saw the remains of a ramshackle, clearly hastily dismantled hideaway half-buried beneath mesquite. His heart was hammering. All the hours he had searched, and now at last a damned wolf had shown him what he sought! But the terrible fear was in him that he was too late.

His hands were shaking as he hunkered down and started where the wolf had left off, scratching away at the soil. Within seconds he made the first grisly discovery of flesh and her name forced its way to his lips . . . 'Altha . . . oh Lord!'

He scraped some more, his fingers clawing frantically at the earth — and then a pig's snout was unearthed, followed by the beast's partly consumed body. The blood rushed from his head and he felt dizzy. Not Altha . . . but Gausman's half-finished meal!

He was shaking his head with disbelief when he came to his feet, but he forced himself to be careful. Gausman might be anywhere around — and so might Altha!

His .44 at the ready, he edged into

the hideaway, stooping low. He found the remnants of ropes, now cut — and he felt sure that this was where Altha had been held captive. But where was she now? Was she still alive?

★ ★ ★

Four frustrating days later Adam boarded the noon stage for Waco. With time passing, Cal Gausman having met his doom and no sign of his sister, Adam felt the only lead he had left lay at the guest-house run by Irma Gausman's sister. Was it possible that Cornelius had followed his wife there — or maybe Irma might have some knowledge of his and Altha's whereabouts.

At the ranch, his stepmother Hannah had become more frantic with concern, but she refused to leave Seth Hardeman's side as he continued his recovery. He was directing much of the work involved in the running of the ranch from his bed. Adam had spent as little time as possible with them, for neither showed him any warmth. Instead, he slept and fed at the bunkhouse when he was at home, though most of his hours were spent searching for his sister. With no new marshal yet appointed at Kwahadi Falls, he felt very much on his own.

So today he was setting out for Waco, but there was little hope in his heart. The awful fear in him was that Altha had been murdered, and her body secreted somewhere in the vastness of the *brasada*. It had been by almost impossible chance that he had eventually stumbled across Gausman's hideaway — but his luck had extended no further. Now, in going to Waco, he knew he was clutching at proverbial straws.

The Concord stage got away on time and before long Adam had concluded that it must have been the most uncomfortable means of transport ever invented. Every bone in the body was getting jarred as the vehicle's four-in-hand team lurched over potholes and rocks at a steady canter. The drivers, using their whips unstintingly, obviously subscribed to the doctrine that time meant money. Front and rear boots and roof-rack were piled high with baggage and mail, while inside six passengers, including two females, suffered in silence, conversation being nigh impossible against the roar of iron-rimmed wheels.

Adam strove to shut his mind to the flow of futile speculation of what lay ahead, and dwelt on sweeter memories. He recalled how he'd stopped off at Kwahadi Springs cemetery and found Kathleen McCrain tending her father's grave, somehow looking cool and pretty in the Texas heat, although still clad in a sombre dress and black bonnet of mourning. She'd given him a smile, reached out and patted his arm as greeting. She was a tactile person, never afraid to touch you, and he enjoyed it.

He wondered if she was aware of his past, aware that he had been convicted of murder. If she was, it certainly did not show in her manner. They had chatted pleasantly for a half-hour, she expressing her sympathy at the mystery surrounding his sister — and afterwards he had walked her home. They passed the square.

'Thank God they've dismantled that awful gallows,' she said. 'I pray they'll never have to use it again.'

He nodded. 'Kathleen, as you know I'm going to Waco. There's just the slight chance Cornelius's wife might still be with her sister, and just might know somethin'. Where can I find her? Waco's a big place.'

Kathleen shook her head, thought for a moment, then said, 'I think her sister runs a guest-house, though just where it is I've no idea.'

They stopped at her garden gate, stood for a moment in the shade of the chinaberry-tree. 'Come in for a while, Adam,' she said. 'It's so good to talk with you.'

'Nothin' would make me happier,' he said, 'but I feel time is slippin' away from me. I can't rest until I find Altha. Every moment I'm not searchin' for her, I feel could cost her her life — if it's not too late already.'

She nodded understandingly, her candid eyes on his. She reached out and grasped his hand. 'When you come back from Waco,' she said, 'maybe you could come for supper.'

'That would be good,' he said, and then he'd left her. She had stirred some emotion inside him that he couldn't explain. She was the first woman, apart from Altha, that he'd really felt deeply about.

The stage stopped at several way stations, the squeal of brakeshoes coming as a pleasing sound, for it heralded respite. The passengers could take welcome refreshment while the horses were changed. One overnight stop was made and next day they arrived in Waco mid-morning, following the Chisholm cattle trail and crossing the newly erected toll-bridge, a magnificent structure suspended on giant hawsers. The town, which had grown up around the ferry, was bedecked with banners and flags for it was celebrating the fact that Texas had been readmitted to the Union after its secession in 1861. The Civil War had brought defeat for the break-away states and, after the war, there had been a period of occupation by federal troops.

But now the yoke of occupation had been withdrawn, Texas was again a fully fledged member of the United States, bitter hostilities forgotten, and there was an air of gay abandon everywhere, with the saloons doing a roaring trade. Already numerous cattle pens had been built and the town awaited the arrival of the railroad, the great iron horse, which was snaking its way northward from Houston and would bring incredible prosperity.

Adam climbed stiffly from the coach. He was travelling light. He stretched the kinks from his limbs and glanced around, reminding himself that he had no idea where he was going to look for the Gausmans. All he had was the vague mention of a guest-house owned by a lady with an unknown name. The sprawling magnitude of the town made his task even more daunting. It was bustling with life, despite the heat. Lines of wagons stood in the main street, Baylor Street, laden to the thoroughbraces with bales of cotton. Waco formed the intermediate trading centre between San Antonio and Dallas. Further along, a quack doctor was peddling his bottled wares, his boasts rising above the babble of voices.

Adam reckoned that the place must be awash with small guest-houses, but any well-organized town should have a registered list of these so maybe the first place to check out was the town marshal's office. He located this by means of a quick enquiry, and was impressed by its size and the array of barred cells at the back end. He could see no sign of any inmates, but a young man with a deputy's badge sat at a desk and Adam asked him if he kept a register of available accommodation. He also asked if the deputy knew a Mrs Gausman but drew a blank.

A moment later he was sitting at a side table scanning down a giant list of boarding-house addresses. There were over a hundred of them and offered no clue as to which one he was seeking. His only means of finding Mrs Gausman was to ask at every establishment — a truly daunting task, almost as overawing as combing through the *brasada*.

Scarcely had he started jotting down names and addresses when a man who had been sitting nearby in the office lowered the newspaper he had been reading, rose and stepped across to Adam. He had large bushy eyebrows and a red face.

'I heard you mentioned the name of Gausman,' he stated.

Adam's interest quickened. 'Sure. She's the sister of a lady who owns a guest-house.'

'I know her,' the stranger announced.

Adam produced a five-dollar bill and slipped into the man's hand.

'Try the Sunrise guest-house, run by Emily Robbins,' he said. 'I know she's got her sister helping her out. It's along Bridge Street on the river's right bank. It's a mighty poor area; they call it Rats' Row, and a smell of garbage hangs about the area, but the guest-house does a good enough job.' He went on to give Adam directions, then added: 'Mention Josh Tasker sent you. She'll be glad enough for the business.'

Adam was overwhelmed with gratitude. He shook the surprised man's hand with gusto. This had been an amazing slice of luck and would save him hours of tedious searching.

Twenty minutes later he had found the guesthouse. True enough the area was run down, but this house looked well kept, with neat lace curtains at the windows and a fine sign proclaiming *Good Food and Clean Bed for Genuine Guests — No Booze or Gunplay.*

The wild hope was in him that Altha might be at this very house. He took a deep breath and knocked, waited impatiently and eventually heard footsteps approaching from within. The door was opened by a woman in a high-necked black gown. She was almost as tall as he was. Her bony face was triangular in shape, her lips pursed. Her grey hair was drawn tight into ear-muffs, but despite her severe appearance there was a touch of timidity about her.

'I'm looking for Mrs Irma Gausman,' he said.

She made no response and he added, 'My name's Adam Ballard and I'm trying to find my sister. I believe she may be with Cornelius Gausman.'

The mention of Cornelius's name brought a sudden widening to her eyes. She hesitated, then said, 'I'm Irma Gausman. I left my husband over a year ago. I couldn't stand his ways. I haven't seen him since and I know nothing of your sister.'

Adam gave her a probing look. 'Is that true?' he asked.

'Y-yes. It's true.'

'You've no idea where I can find him, then?'

She shook her head. 'I'm sorry.'

Before he could say any more she closed the door, leaving him slack jawed.

He stood, racking his brain for further ideas. Instinct told him that she was lying. She'd been altogether too anxious to terminate the conversation. For a moment he was daunted by the thought that he had never seen Cornelius Gausman, so he would not recognize him even if he came face to face with him. But then he recalled that at least he'd been afforded a brief glimpse of his twin brother as he'd left the Kwahadi Springs prior to his trial. Any resemblance would give him some clue.

On the opposite side of the street was a rubbish patch littered by a number of empty boxes and assorted trash amid which several stray dogs were rummaging. It was late afternoon now, the sun beginning to slip into its westward drift. He would need accommodation himself shortly, but firstly he decided to spy out on the house for a while. He crossed the street, concealed himself as best he could. He watched the windows of the house and presently saw an upstairs curtain twitch before being drawn slightly aside. He made sure he was unobserved and shortly the curtain dropped back into place. A few minutes later a boy of about fifteen left the house, glanced around and set off up the street, the urgent speed of his pace indicating that he was on a mission.

Adam followed him through a maze of back alleyways, fearing more than once that he'd lost him, but somehow he kept on his trail and ten minutes or so later they reached the main thoroughfare of the town, and even more to the point a saloon called *Jezebel's Rest*. The boy entered without hesitation and Adam sauntered in his wake, stepping inside to be greeted by the raucous murmur of voices and clink of glasses.

The bar-room was crowded with cowboys, freighters and townsmen, with a scattering of saloon women in gaudy dress, and four green-topped tables at which poker was being played. In the background he could hear the rattle of a roulette wheel. The whole place was fragrant with rough-cut and burley. Adam's attention was drawn to where the boy was in earnest conversation with a scrawny, stoop-shouldered individual who was sitting alone at a table. Adam was convinced that this was Cornelius Gausman and the pulse was suddenly drumming in his temple. The boy had obviously come to carry warning.

Cornelius had shaved off his beard, leaving an untidy stubble, but there was no mistaking the high forehead, prominent brows and deep-set eyes. In front of him was a half-finished bottle of whiskey. He'd clearly been drinking heavily.

Adam loosened his .44 in its holster. He prayed there would be no gunplay; the place was crowded and bullets would cause mayhem, but he knew he must be prepared.

He threaded his way through drinkers until he was standing close behind Gausman, then in a firm voice he said: 'Cornelius Gausman. Where's my sister?'

The aggressiveness of his demand brought a cessation to the burble of conversation about him, a shifting back from the immediate vicinity. The boy watched with wide, frightened eyes.

Almost casually Gausman turned his head, met Adam's cold stare.

'My sister?' Adam repeated. 'Where is she?'

'Don't know what you're talkin' about,' Gausman said, his voice slurred.

'You know what I'm talkin' about,' Adam persisted. 'You know how you kidnapped her, how your brother swung and how you should have been alongside him. Now I want to know what you've done with my sister. All I can say is that you better not have harmed her.'

There was a surprised titter of voices from the onlookers, but many sensed the growing sense of menace that had arisen and there was a further backing away.

'I'll ask you again,' Adam demanded. 'Where is she?'

Gausman glanced nervously around, licking his lips. He knew that both men and women were hanging on his words. He was no more a popular member of the community here than he had been in his home town. Few knew who he was or where he came from, but now he found himself the focus of attention and anger brought an additional flush to his face. He felt cornered and sensed that Adam was not going to back down.

He took a shuddering breath, then said, 'I didn't harm her. I let her go!'

Adam's impatience was growing. 'You're lyin',' he said. 'Where is she?'

'I'm not lyin',' Gausman countered, though he clearly sensed that nobody believed him. His murky eyes were boiling with hate.

'Then I shall send for the marshal,' Adam said. 'You can do your explainin' to him.' He turned towards the watching throng, seeking a volunteer to bring in the law.

That was the moment when the fury seemed to overflow in Gausman and he cried out: 'Goddam you!'

The crowd sensed what was coming and women were screaming as he went for his gun, carrying the briefest warning to Adam, enabling him to duck and twist away as Gausman hoisted himself to his feet and yanked his gun clear of its holster. Its blast filled the room.

There was a mad confusion, a rush of chairs and tables being overturned, of people stumbling, shouting, screaming, glasses, bottles scattering.

The bullet had passed through the brim of Adam's Stetson, but Gausman was thumbing back the hammer for a second shot. Adam's own gun leapt into his fist, the speed engendered by a hundred practices, making it appear no more than a blur. Its detonation came like a delayed echo of the first but it was quick enough to forestall further bullets. A bloodied hole showed briefly between Gausman's eyes, then he fell backwards, splintering the table in his downward plunge.

Adam glanced desperately around, his ears singing with the blast trapped in confined space. He felt sick and in desperate need of air amid the odour of burned powder. He'd had no wish for matters to turn out this way, but to his knowledge nobody other than Gausman had suffered. For this he thanked God. He had fired purely on reflex and now he slipped his still-smoking gun back into its leather and somebody was calling out for calm.

Several men and a woman crouched down beside the fallen Gausman but they soon rose shaking their heads. Even if they'd wished to restore him to life, there was nothing they could do.

He would never again indulge in criminality, at least not in this world — nor would he ever reveal any secrets that had been in his mind.

A tot of whiskey was thrust into Adam's hand with the advice: 'Drink up and get out o' Waco quick!' He found he was shaking so much that he had to toss the drink back in one gulp, otherwise it would have been spilled.

He knew that but for whiskey events would have been very different. First, it was liquor that had caused anger to erupt within this man he had trailed — and second, Gausman's aim would have been truer had he not been drunk. He would probably also still be alive.

For a moment Adam reproached himself. Irma Gausman must have had some regard for her husband otherwise she would have not sent a message to warn him. In so doing, she had, unknowingly, brought about his downfall. But then Adam's thoughts swung to Altha and his bitterness against the man who had kidnapped her and subjected her to who knew what, banished regrets from him.

He took a final glance at the man he had killed, seeing him as a pathetic, crumpled skunk of whom the world was well rid. He turned to move away, to cleave a path through those who stood gawking, the taint of gunsmoke still hanging in the air, but then he became aware that several newcomers had entered the saloon.

Foremost was a tall, upright man with a handlebar moustache. A marshal's badge was pinned to his beaded, buckskin vest. He stood with his hand rested upon the butt of his holstered pistol. 'Hold still, mister,' he said to Adam in a voice which overrode all other sound. 'I'm arresting you on a charge of killing this man!'

His deputies formed a crescent behind him, blocking any means of retreat.

7

It had been four days earlier, or more precisely four nights, that Altha Ballard had ridden through the tangled thickets of the *brasada*, following the glint of the river by moonlight. Her mind struggled with the knowledge that she was still alive, though sometimes she wondered if death was a form of madness and she had stepped over this threshold. But she could feel the cold bite of the night air on her body. The tangled remnants of her dress did little to shield her. And such feeling seemed akin to life and she had to conclude that the mind of Cornelius Gausman was more garbled than her own.

To have the muzzle of a gun inches from your head, to be conscious of the gnarled finger of a madman tightening on the trigger and be ready for the step into the next world, there to confront the Lord's infinite compassion and understanding — and then suddenly for everything to change was enough to propel anybody into insanity.

As she reached the sloping bank of the river and followed along close to the water, her mind wrestled with Gausman's macabre behaviour. In a weird, frenzied voice he'd explained his brother's terrible death in such vivid terms that she was sharing with him every second of the horror — the crazed eyes as the rope constricted about his throat, the choking, gagging, hopeless efforts to relieve the strangle. As Cornelius spoke, or rather slathered over his words, the anger in him seemed to increase and the muzzle of the gun wavered before her like the head of some evil serpent; he had cursed all those who were associated with the Double-X whom he held to blame for all his troubles, and he swore how his vengeance must now focus on this crazy girl he held captive. Once his finger compressed the trigger of his gun, her head would be nigh blown from her shoulders.

'Do it!' she had repeated like a challenge, 'then they can hang you too!'

* * *

The horse was flagging. She reined in and sat listening as its blowing gradually steadied until eventually it dipped its muzzle into the river and drew up water. She shivered. Why was she alive? She tried to reason it out.

The face was that her words about his hanging had seemed to strike home. He knew a man could swing for mavericking, even kidnapping — but death was by no means mandatory and often depended on the whim of the judge. It must have been sheer fear, absolute horror at the thought of suffering the same fate as his brother Cal, that had made him suddenly lower the gun and turn away, gazing up through the tangled branches at the sky.

When eventually his voice had come,

it was little more than a whisper: 'Damn you and all your kind!'

He swung back towards her and slapped her face with the back of his hand. She felt the skin burst open and knew she had an ugly welt on her cheek.

'Why don't you cringe and crawl?' he shouted. 'Why are you always so damned indifferent to me!'

Again he appeared to lapse into inner turmoil, then he seemed to make up his mind. He drew his skinning-knife from the scabbard at his belt, stooped so close she could smell his breath; then he cut her ropes.

'Get out of my sight,' he hissed.

She stirred her stiffened limbs, scarcely believing her ears.

'Get away from me!' he shouted, insanity blazing from his deep-set eyes.

Her voice came almost matter of fact. 'On foot, I shall get lost in the *brasada*. I'll never find my way out.'

He made an impatient growling sound. 'There's two horses tethered in the brush. Take one, follow down the draw till you reach the river, follow it to the fork, after that strike out across the meadows towards the distant line of hills. Keep going for an hour, then you'll hit the Kwahadi River and follow it downstream into town. Tell them that old Cornelius wasn't all bad, that he let you go even though you didn't deserve it.'

She nodded, speechless, then she stumbled away and found the horses — two wiry mustangs. Despite his instructions, she'd be lucky not to get lost in the coming darkness. But did anything matter now? She found the saddles lying close to the animals and got one across the back of the smaller beast. She tightened the cinch, slipped the bridle into place. She could hear Cornelius thrashing about angrily in the brush behind her. Was he changing his mind? She didn't linger to find out, but mounted up and kneed the mustang into a trot.

Even if she did lose her way, and with

darkness deepening by the minute that was highly likely, the mustang would not. He would be anxious to get out of the *brasada* into his home meadows.

It was well into the small hours when she eventually came clear of the Big Thicket and was on familiar ground. But she had no intention of going home, nor of entering the night-shrouded town. Instead she rode northward. Dawn was tinging the eastern sky when she reached Walnut Canyon, shadowed and dark now. Near the opening to the canyon, on the banks of a stream and sheltered by a grove of cotton-woods, stood a single cabin — well appointed, stone-walled, solid. No light showed from it, but she threw herself from her mount, her heart hammering fiercely.

This was the home of Kirk Steckline.

Without hesitation she stepped up on to the stoop and hammered with her fists upon the door. There was no response. She repeated the hammering with growing desperation. At last a lantern flared from within and she heard his voice call: 'Who's there!'

'Altha,' she responded, and there came the sound of bolts being drawn back and the tall outline of Kirk Steckline was silhouetted in the doorway.

'What the . . . ?'

'I've come to you, Kirk,' she gasped. 'I've come to you because I need help . . . and because I'm carrying your baby!'

Back in the cabin, in Steckline's bed, a young Mexican woman, Lucia Cabellero, heard the voices and slipped from beneath the blanket. By the time Altha was inside the cabin's main room, she was in the kitchen as any normal housekeeper might have been.

'You've got to hide me,' Altha was saying. 'I can't go home . . . ever!'

Steckline sighed. This wasn't part of his plan. He cursed the dalliance he'd had with the girl. He cursed the time that he had met her in church, found her strangely attractive despite her paleness and invited her out for several Sunday afternoon rides. At first he was fascinated by her in her green riding-habit with divided skirt, man's hickory shirt and pert straw hat. Her small breasts attracted him. One thing had led to another; he even delighted in stripping naked and insisting she whip him with her riding crop. But gradually he tired of her and he felt he'd made it clear that their relationship was over. He now wondered if her claim of pregnancy was a ploy. For the moment, however, he reckoned he had no alternative but to go along with her plea.

★　★　★

When Adam had taken a casual glance at the cells lining the back of the marshal's office in Waco earlier in the day, he had little anticipated that before nightfall he would be an inmate himself. But the fact was that he found himself relieved of his gun and frog-marched out of *Jezebel's Rest* and along the street to Marshal John Rimmer's establishment and locked behind bars, the cell door clanging with awesome finality. He sank on to the narrow wooden cot, an icy despair cutting him to the marrow. The prospect of being placed on trial for the murder of Cornelius Gausman appalled him, for he had already suffered such an injustice and endured eight years in the harshest of penitentiaries for a crime he had not committed — and with a previous sentence for murder on his record he would be branded a violent man and as such punished accordingly.

That evening one of Rimmer's deputies visited him and took down a statement. Adam gave the fullest account possible, including the events at Kwahadi Springs and his reasons for coming to Waco. He was served some basic food with a big mug of water and then left to his own thoughts. Surely what he was suffering was an annoying interlude which, come morning, would be put right and his freedom restored — but a nagging doubt persisted in his mind. Injustices had occurred before, as well he knew.

And all the while, pestering him like a recalcitrant dog, was the belief that he was no nearer finding Altha than he had ever been.

For hours he lay listening to the drunken shouts of inmates in other cells and the comings and goings in the outside office, but eventually he lapsed into sleep. When he awoke light was streaming through the bars of the outside window. Presently he was supplied with a bowl of cold water in which he refreshed himself and about an hour later he was visited by none other than Marshal Rimmer himself.

'We questioned Irma Gausman about your sister,' he said, seating himself on the end of the bunk, 'and she denied all knowledge of her. She said her husband had turned up in a harassed state and she knew he had been up to no good, but long ago she had given up asking him about his activities. He'd been glad enough to find refuge at the guest-house, but said he'd be moving on in a few days and that after that he wouldn't be troubling her any more. I'm sure she was telling the truth.'

Adam nodded, disappointed that Rimmer had been unable to unearth any further evidence regarding Altha's fate.

'Funny thing is,' the marshal contin-ued, 'the woman seemed quite cut up about her husband's death despite admitting that he was the blackest scoundrel on earth.'

'Marshal,' Adam said, 'I'm desperate to find my sister. Every second I spend kicking my heels locked up here, she may be one step nearer the grave. I didn't come to Waco with intention of killing anybody, but Gausman gave me no option. He was preparing for a second shot when I drew on him. I don't think he'd have missed at the second attempt. The first shot was close enough.'

Rimmer nodded. 'I saw the hole in your hat. Anyway, I've questioned around and everybody who saw the incident agrees that you acted in self-defence. No one's fault but Gausman's hisself. So you can collect your gun and be on your way. I don't think you'll find your sister here, but if I come across any clue I'll telegraph the marshal at Kwahadi Springs.'

Adam grunted with the relief of freedom. By noon that day he was aboard the stage, homeward bound, having gained little by visiting Waco apart from the knowledge that Cornelius Gausman would no longer play a part in his investigations.

8

'You've heard who the new marshal of Kwahadi Springs is?' Kathleen McCrain enquired as she ladled some stew on to Adam's plate. It was two evenings later and he was seated in her parlour, having accepted her invitation to a candle-lit supper. He liked the cosy, warm glow of the room with a giltframed photograph of her late father on the dresser.

'No,' he said. 'I haven't heard.'

'Kirk Steckline. The town council were really anxious to fill the post quickly and figured he was the ideal candidate.'

'Kirk Steckline?' Adam queried. 'Don't think I know him.'

Kathleen had really made a big do of his visit and had prepared a hearty meal, topped off with fruit dessert and her special cookies, all washed down with a bottle of wine.

'Steckline always reckoned he was a handsome hunk,' she explained, 'handy with a gun. He worked as a cowhand at the Diamond Horseshoe ranch on a part-time basis, but didn't have much to do with the other men. He owns a cabin up near Walnut Canyon, spends most of his time there. It's a pretty smart place, not like an average cowhand's shack.'

Adam nodded, tucking into his meal. 'Well, I hope he'll do a good job. I better let him know in the morning what happened at Waco. One less mavericker for him to attend to.'

He pondered for a moment, then said: 'Kathleen, do you know the truth about me, that I served eight years in prison for murder?'

'I heard, but that's in the past. I don't know the circumstances but it's none of my business. You've served your time and it's all behind you now. You don't seem like a cold-blooded killer to me, Adam.'

'I'd like you to know the truth,' he said.

'You don't have to explain anything to me. I'm more than happy to accept you as you are now. I know you're not a bad man.'

He smiled at her trust, but then grew serious. 'I'd like you to know what happened.'

She sighed. 'All right. If it'll help you, I'll listen.'

'I didn't hit things off too well with my father,' he explained. 'I guess I was a headstrong kid and he wouldn't take my sassing and as I grew up he used the strap on me more times than I care to say. Even so, lookin' back, I realize that he figured what he did was for my own good, and deep down, although it didn't seem so, we were fond of each other.'

She nodded understandingly, her eyes on his.

'The truth was we had some almighty shouting matches and I used to storm off and sulk. Thank God I've grown out of that. I used to take off with my dog Risker and walk for miles. Anyway, as I got older, I pulled my weight on the ranch he'd started to build and I guess we worked well enough together.

'Then when I'd just turned sixteen, the dog Risker took sick. I was real fond of him, nursed him like a child I guess. But one day when I had my back turned, Pa fired a bullet into his head, putting him out of his misery, as he put it. I went crazy, swearin' he wasn't sick enough to be put down — but Pa wouldn't have it and our tempers flared and we ranted and raved at each other, almost came to blows. I buried Risker up on the side of the valley where he'd roamed so often. His grave's still there, I guess.'

He paused, wondering if she was growing tired of his tale but she said, 'Go on, Adam.'

'Well, Pa and me were due to go out branding that morning. I'll admit we were in pretty bad humour with each other. Our ranting had given way to silence. We didn't talk as we rode, just glared at each other. We were well into the *brasada*, had located a number of calves for branding, had started the fire and were getting ready to rope them. It was then that somebody fired from the cover of the mesquite and I suddenly realized that Pa had gone down and there was blood all over his head. I heard somebody moving in the brush, drew my gun and fired at the sound. I wasn't sure if I'd hit anybody, but later I found blood in the mesquite. I checked Pa, realized he was dead, half his head shot away. I rushed into the brush, trying to find whoever fired the shot, but there was no trace.'

Kathleen pursed her lips in sympathy. 'Poor Adam.'

'Well, after I'd reported what had happened, I was arrested and charged with Pa's murder. Nobody believed my story. They even claimed I'd planted some of my father's blood in the mesquite to give the impression that somebody else had fired a shot. Pa's foreman Seth Hardeman stood up in the courtroom and told about the flaming row we'd had and how murder had blazed from my eyes. Hardeman and me had always disliked each other. I suppose I've got to admit that jealousy came into it. Maybe he saw it as a way of getting rid of me. Maybe he had designs on my stepmother even then.'

Kathleen drew in her breath sibilantly.

'Could be the judge had some doubt in his mind,' Adam continued. 'I don't know. He could have sentenced me to the rope, but he was lenient. He said he was letting me off light because I was a youngster and sentenced me to jail. Nobody has ever believed my side of the story.'

'I believe you, Adam,' she murmured gently.

They lapsed into silence; the telling of the story had sobered them.

Presently she reached out and rested her hand on his. 'Thank you for tellin' me, Adam.'

The light was softening and he looked at this girl and realized how much he appreciated her understanding, her trust. Sitting with her, he felt more at home than he had ever done before in his life. After a moment he slipped his arm about her shoulder and she rested her head upon his chest and he no longer seemed an outcast. When it was time to go, she brought him his hat and fingered the hole in the brim where Gausman's bullet had gone through.

'You've got to be careful,' she said. 'I wouldn't want anythin' to happen to you, Adam.'

'Well, Cornelius won't trouble me any more, that's a sure thing.' His voice came with no pride. There could be no pleasure in killing a man, not even one as bad as Gausman — and with the killing he had destroyed his one certain source of information about Altha. But he'd had little option.

She led the way out into the warm night and they stood in the starlight.

Suddenly the clutch of her hand tightened on his arm and they came together in a sudden embrace, her breasts firm against him. The wine had softened their inhibitions. Her lips were warm and hungry and when she drew back for breath, she was laughing.

'I thought it would never happen,' she murmured.

He kissed her again, savouring the taste of her mouth, and whispered, 'Thanks, honey, for a lovely evenin',' knowing that she was a woman with the warmest of hearts.

When he turned away, he felt that his face was on fire; he was apprehensive at what might have happened had he lingered but he was filled with exhilaration nonetheless.

*　*　*

Kirk Steckline had no religious convictions — in fact quite the reverse. He believed that a man had to look out for himself in this life and grab all he could. Even so he'd cultivated the habit of regular church attendance for a distinct purpose: to establish a reputation as an upstanding member of the Kwahadi Springs community. He'd long held ambitions to assume the post of town marshal, not because of the modest salary it attracted, but because it would provide the perfect shield for his other activities. The real money was to be made from mavericking and he'd been a willing partner in the Gausmans' enterprises, the sound structure and comfortable accommodation of his cabin at Walnut Canyon being ample confirmation of this. Perhaps some folk wondered how a casual cowhand working for the Diamond Horseshoe outfit could afford such a place, and that was why he needed an appointment which offered a regular income to cover his more lucrative source of revenue — the sale of illegally branded hides.

Even had Amos McCrain not passed away from natural causes, his health had been in such a delicate state of late that his retirement was inevitable. His death had merely hastened events. Nobody on the town council had opposed Steckline as replacement. Maybe the handsome blond was brash, cultivated his boxcar moustache with extreme vanity, wore somewhat gaudy clothes and walked with a macho swagger, but that was of little importance compared with the fact that he knew how to use his gun.

Now he leaned back in his office chair and reckoned that his new appointment would make few demands on him. Just the occasional drunkard, whom he was quite capable of throwing into the town jail if the occasion demanded, and he would leave any maverickers in the territory, including himself, to attend to their business undeterred.

As marshal, he'd received a telegram from Waco this very morning reporting the death of Cornelius. He regretted the deaths of the Gausmans not because he harboured any affection for them, but because the twins had been good organizers, provided a useful cog in his intrigues, and knew certain intricate passageways through the *brasada*. In the event of things going wrong, such as had happened when Seth Hardeman and his Double-X crew had caught them red-handed, they were obvious targets to carry the blame. Thank goodness he'd hoisted his bandanna into place in time to avoid recognition.

But there was another reason Steckline mourned Cornelius. Cornelius owed him money. In fact within the hour he would be on his way to the Gausman homestead to see if he could find any stashed-away cash.

The fact was that Steckline had every reason to feel pleased with himself for having gained a position of respect in town. This would deflect from him any suspicion for future misdeeds and also enable him to manipulate to his own advantage any investigations which followed.

But one thing had threatened the success of his plans, and that was the arrival of the girl. He now wondered what he had ever seen in her as she sang devoutly in church. Beyond her physical attraction, perhaps it had been the prospect of destroying her primness. But when he had deflowered her that spring day amid the meadow grasses, he had overlooked the fact that his seed might take root, that he might be lumbered with far more than he bargained for.

And now she had thrown herself on his mercy, and if he turned her out she could blow everything he'd planned sky high. He decided he might well have to complete the task that Cornelius had flinched from — and put an end to the unstable creature. Alternatively, he could take the extreme step of marrying her, but the thought made him frown. His brief though intimate association with her destroyed all appeal of such action. Furthermore, he was comfortable with the Mexican woman Lucinda

Cabellero to act as housekeeper and bedmate. In the latter role, she gave him everything he needed, and in all other respects she made few demands on him, accepting his unexplained absences and other activities without question. He had never met her family, nor had he any desire to do so.

Now he had two women in his household, two women whom he had expected to despise each other, but strangely this had not been the case. Contrary to everything he had expected, they had struck up a friendship.

But now he had to turn his mind to other things: the money owed him by the Gausmans. He locked up his office, leaving a note on the door saying he would return next day, collected his horse from the livery and rode out of town.

*   *   *

Adam had no knowledge of Kirk Steckline nor his background. All he knew was that he was the new marshal and that he would seek help from him in tracking down the whereabouts of his sister Altha. But when he reached the office, it was to find the place closed. Steckline had left no indication of his destination.

Adam was growing increasingly desperate, imbued with the feeling that the sands of time were running out on him. Was it possible that Gausman had been telling the truth when he'd claimed that he had released Altha unharmed? If so, why hadn't she appeared? He pondered for a long moment. There was always the grim possibility that Cornelius had killed her and buried her in a less obvious place in the *brasada* than the grave he had chosen for the half-devoured pig.

Presently he made up his mind. He would ride out to Walnut Canyon, see if Steckline had gone home and was willing to co-operate in planning future strategy.

The town simmered in the noon sun as he rode down Main Street; everywhere was quiet and he had the forlorn feeling that life had lapsed back to normality following the drama of the trial and hanging. Also plaguing him was the feeling that the disappearance of his sister would soon be forgotten and life would go on as if nothing had happened. Altha would be forgotten, her fate a mystery that would never be solved — unless he persisted in probing, in reminding people. Cornelius Gausman could no longer be punished for his crimes, but there must be other men who knew what had become of her and whether she still survived.

It was an hour's ride to Walnut Canyon. He passed isolated homesteads and farms but the only sign of life he encountered came from the odd woman hanging out washing or a farmer hoeing his crops. The land was large, virgin, absorbing man's meagre attempts to populate. Most of the Indian tribes had moved north into the Staked Plains where the buffalo on which they depended still abounded — but he knew times would change. One day there would be mass migration of whites from the overcrowded East and everything would be different, particularly as Texas had been readmitted to the Union.

At last he reached the red sandstone cliff faces where the canyons opened out into the flatter terrain of meadow and desert. He knew when he reached Walnut Canyon, so named because of the colouring of its rock walls. At its lower end was the solid structure of Steckline's cabin. True enough, it was very different from the average shack or dog-house with its stone walls and well-appointed windows — vastly different from the hovel in which the Gausmans had lived. The Gausmans had had money from their ill-gotten gains, but had never shaken off their laziness, or maybe they'd considered that any show of wealth would have brought a finger of suspicion pointing in their direction.

Adam saw no smoke rising from the Steckline chimney, so that meant no cooking was in progress. There was no washing on the line and the whole place was dead quiet, which made him wonder if his journey had been wasted. Some yards back he reined in his bay horse and surveyed the place. It never paid to go sashaying in when visiting, for fear of attracting a bullet, so he cupped his hands to his mouth and called out a greeting. The sound came back to him from the distant cliff face in mocking echo. He touched his heels to his animal's flanks and went forward. He wondered why he was feeling so apprehensive. After all, he was visiting the town marshal, yet an uneasiness persisted in him.

Twenty yards back from the cabin he halted and slipped from his saddle, leaving his animal at a watertrough. He stepped up on to the stoop, called again, then knocked on the door. There was no response, only a sound of emptiness from within. He had to face facts. Marshal Steckline was not at home.

Sighing with frustration, he peered in through a window, seeing a neat room within, an indication of a woman's touch. But he could see no sign that Steckline had been in residence recently. He slapped his thigh with annoyance, then, as he gazed through the window, he saw something that made his blood freeze, something wholly familiar to him.

On the table was a crimson shawl — and he had only ever seen one quite like this. It was the shawl he had given Altha when he first returned. The blood was suddenly pounding in his temples. What was it doing here? He returned to the main door of the place, raised the latch and to his surprise the door swung open.

He was greeted by the buzz of flies coming from an inner room — a bedroom, and he felt an increasing sense of unease. He went through the main room and into the bedroom. There he beheld a vision of something most horrible, something he had feared for so long.

Altha was lying on the bed, her head

a mass of blood, yet her great eyes still gazed at him. Her arm was stretched downward and on the floor beneath her hand was a pistol.

9

For a moment he stood stunned. At last he paced forward, stood directly over her, half-believing that she might show some sign of life, but she did not and he knew she was gone for ever. He wanted to vomit, but somehow he held tight on his guts. Everything he'd striven for, all his efforts to find her, had been wasted — and suddenly he unleashed a great wail of anguish.

His thoughts, his anger, swung towards Steckline. What did he know about this? The pistol lying on the floor beside the bed; it could have dropped from her hand as she blew her own brains out — or it could have been planted by her murderer to give the impression of suicide.

Whatever had happened, Kirk Steckline had a lot of explaining to do.

He wanted to reach out, to take Altha

in his arms and bring the warmth of life back into her poor body, but he did not. Instead, he turned, determined to find Steckline and demand from him an explanation.

Blinded by his emotions, he had stepped out on to the stoop when the heavy-calibre shot came, making an echoing boom. His immediate reaction was to duck down behind the inadequate cover that the rail of the stoop provided. A bullet had splintered shards of wood from the down-sloping roof, inches above where his head had been. His senses were hammering in the expectation of a further shot. A trickle of sweat coasted down beneath his shirt. At first he thought it was blood, then discovered it was not. He estimated that the shot had come from the fringe of trees some twenty yards to his left. For a moment he laid in a protective curled position, hands cupped to his head, then he realized the futility of this. Gingerly he raised his eyes and peered in the direction from which the shot had come.

Nothing moved in the trees, and in the yard in front of the cabin his bay horse had calmed and was gazing at him with enquiring eyes. Crouching low, he edged to the corner of the cabin, expecting at any moment to hear the blast and perhaps feel the crippling impact of another shot — but nothing came. Once behind the cover of the cabin corner, he paused to take stock.

The shot had been too close for comfort. It was the second time within the last few days that deadly lead had cleaved the air within inches of his head. How much longer could his luck hold out?

For a moment, in his scramble to avoid being shot, he had forgotten the terrible discovery he had made in the cabin — now it returned to him and with it an overwhelming sense of depression. What had driven Altha to her death, and had it been by her own hand, or contrived by somebody else? Steckline? If so, why?

And was it Steckline who had taken a

shot at him? Some inner instinct told him that it had not been he. But whoever it was, he had to track the marshal down and extract an explanation.

He had no desire to linger here at the cabin. Another shot could come at any time. He risked a further gaze in the direction of the trees, but the only movement he saw came from the stirring of the branches in the breeze. He glanced at his horse. The animal, sensing his gaze, nickered to him, impatiently flicking flies from its flanks with its tail. He knew that there was nothing he could do to help his sister now, save bring to justice those who had perpetrated her demise. And perhaps arrange for a wagon to collect her body and convey it to the local undertaker. He shuddered as he thought of the mental and physical turmoil she must have suffered.

He straightened up, drew his gun and walked boldly across the open space towards his horse, keeping his eyes on the trees from which the shot had come, ready at the first sign of danger to plunge to the side. Whoever had fired the shot hadn't shown much persistence. He reached his animal, smoothed its withers with a calming hand, then slipped his foot into the stirrup and swung into the saddle. He had no desire to search around for his assailant. He might still be lurking. Adam decided he would ride back to town, confront Steckline if he was there, if not report matters to the mayor and attempt to recruit his assistance. In his mind, Steckline was completely discredited. It seemed no explanation could alter the fact that Altha's body had been found in his cabin. What was she doing there? In the absence of any proper law in Kwahadi Springs, it might be a matter of bringing in the county sheriff until more satisfactory local law enforcement could be established.

Adam rode with a heavy heart. *Altha is dead.* In desperation he tried to draw the nightmare fragments of this knowledge into some sort of meaning. By the time he reached town sunset had faded to grey twilight and the gaunt fingers of evening shadows darkened horse and rider. The place was stirring into its night life, with the saloons showing signs of activity. From one came a woman's voice rendering *Sweet Afton*.

He went directly to the marshal's office from which the soft spill of lamplight showed through the window. A feeling of grim satisfaction settled in on him; at least, it seemed, Steckline was here and now the time had come for him to provide an explanation.

His pulse quickening, Adam dismounted and hitched his bay horse to the rail. He loosened his gun in its leather, mounted the steps to the stoop and walked in through the open door of the office. The blond man he took to be Steckline was sitting in a swivel-chair, his calico shirt open at the throat, his feet on his roll-top desk, fanning himself with a folded newspaper. He immediately looked up to meet Adam's eye — 'a handsome hunk' as Kathleen had described him, with a neat boxcar moustache.

'Kirk Steckline?' Adam demanded.

'That's me. Why?'

'I just been over to your place in Walnut Canyon,' Adam explained. 'I'm Adam Ballard. I found my sister there. You may recall she was kidnapped a week or so ago?'

Steckline's jaw sagged.

'She was dead.' Adam almost choked on the words.

'Dead!' Steckline was suddenly on his feet, shock, either genuine or faked, was stamped across his face. 'Goddamit it! I don't know what you're talkin' about, Ballard!'

'I'm talking about the truth. The door wasn't locked. I walked into the place and my sister was lying on a bed, her head shot to pieces.'

Steckline looked sickened, but he still managed to say: 'You're lyin'.'

'I'm not lyin',' Adam countered. 'First of all, I want to know what she was doing there.'

Steckline glanced about anxiously as if to make certain they were not overheard. He walked around his desk and closed the door. Adam noticed he wore his gun on his left side, butt-forward, obviously favouring a cross-draw.

'Sit down,' he said. 'Have a cigar. Who do you think shot her?'

He shoved a box of cigars across his desk which Adam ignored.

'I'll stay standing,' he responded. 'I want a quick answer.'

'Who do you think shot her?' Steckline repeated.

'I don't know,' Adam said, 'but I do know you got a powerful lot of explaining to do.'

Steckline frowned, then he started to speak slowly as if choosing his words carefully. 'Your sister and I were very fond of each other. We used to go to church together, went out ridin' on the range in each other's company. I guess we made each other happy. I was shocked and sorry to hear about the kidnap. Anyway, last Thursday she turned up at my cabin in the middle of the night. She was in a right agitated state. She said Cornelius Gausman had let her go — '

'Let her go . . . ' Adam registered his surprise. So the old scoundrel had been telling the truth — but of course he had had no right to kidnap her in the first place.

'He obviously went to his wife in Waco, but I got a telegram this mornin' from the marshal there, a circular telegram to all the law offices in the territory. Gausman was shot in a gunfight, but I suspect you know more about that than I do.'

'Go on,' Adam prompted.

'Well, like I said, she claimed Gausman had let her go. He'd been holding her in the *brasada*. She rode to my place and begged me to take her in, to hide her for a while. She said she just couldn't go home after . . . all that had happened.'

'All that had happened?' Adam queried.

'Sure. She said I was the only one she could turn to. I swear it. That's what I did. I gave the poor girl shelter. What else could I do? After all we'd meant to each other?'

'Then why is she dead, Kirk Steckline?'

He gave his head a despairing shake. 'I just don't know. All I can say she seemed right depressed but . . . '

'You're tellin' me you didn't kill her?'

He gave Adam a fierce look. 'Of course I didn't damn well kill her. I had no reason to.'

'Then who shot her?'

'She must've done it herself,' Steckline said. He gave an agitated shrug. 'Look, I've got a buckboard out the back. You wait here while I fetch it, then we'll ride out to my place and bring her body into the undertaker's. That's the least we can do.'

Adam nodded. Steckline was right. They couldn't leave her body lying out there in an unlocked cabin. It wasn't right.

'I'll put my horse into the livery.' Adam nodded. 'He's worn out. We'll meet back here in five minutes.'

'Sure,' Steckline said, 'but best keep quiet about this. We don't want to stir the whole town up until we've established a few facts.'

Adam reluctantly agreed. He felt he had to play along with this man for the moment, although he didn't trust him further than a grasshopper could spit.

Adam led his horse over to the livery barn. The hostler wasn't around, but Adam placed his animal in an empty stall with an ample supply of oats and water and knew he could sort things out later. He then returned to the marshal's office. Steckline was waiting outside, seated on his buckboard wagon, ready to move off. As they drove out of town, the night was closing in about them.

'I'll have to move into town,' Steckline remarked. 'There's a room over the top of the office. A marshal needs to be on hand.'

Adam didn't comment. How could the man act as if nothing had happened, as if Altha wasn't lying out at his place with the flies buzzing about her corpse and a hundred questions that had to be explained away? Did Steckline not imagine that within a few hours he might no longer be deemed fit to uphold the law, that he might himself be facing a charge of murder or at least of hampering justice?

The miles slipped behind them along the deserted trail, a succession of humpy dunes winding between rocky outcrops; the only sign of light came from a distant homestead and the moon. Somewhere, far off, an owl was sending its mournful cry into the night. It occurred to Adam that he should have left some word in Kwahadi as to what had happened and where he was headed, but now it was too late and he would have to fend for himself. If there was anybody else who knew of Altha's death, then he did not know who it would be — unless it was the person who had shot at him. He was pretty sure it hadn't been Steckline. He had given the appearance of having been in his office for some time. But there was something about the marshal's arrogant manner that he disliked intensely and Steckline might well consider it in his interests to silence Adam in some way. Any scandal over Altha could blow his ambitions to remain as town marshal apart. With this in mind, he watched Steckline's hands with absolute concentration. While they were on the reins of the wagon he felt safe, but out here in the lonely night anything could happen.

There was no conversation between them now. Talk was always difficult in a wagon that was being driven at speed along a rough trail. Adam sat steeped in his own grim thoughts and the macabre prospect of what awaited at the cabin, aware that sooner or later he would have to tell his stepmother what had happened. But despite this he kept his senses on razor's edge.

At a point where the way rose

between high sand-stone rocks and a plunging drop into a brush-clogged crevice, Steckline casually slipped his right hand from the reins and surreptitiously edged it across his lap towards his left-slung gun. As his casualness suddenly changed to darting movement, Adam was ready and he threw his weight against the marshal, drawing his own gun in the same instant. But the pair were too close to raise their weapons and their arms locked in a struggle for supremacy. Steckline's gun did in fact blast off but the lead winged harmlessly into the sky. Adam glimpsed his opponent's grimacing features, the snarling glint of his teeth and he knew that he was fighting for his life. But he had forestalled Steckline's immediate intention.

The wagon was all at once out of control, the shot having panicked the horse, and they swayed back and forth across the trail, gathering speed, coming perilously close to the edge where the ground dipped away into a deep ravine.

Steckline had somehow got his big hands around Adam's throat, was squeezing tight, but Adam thrust upward with his arms, forcing him away. Steckline's boots were hammering into Adam's shins, but Adam brought his knee up into the man's groin — and it was at that moment that the wagon careered off the trail, its wheels losing purchase. It took an abrupt plunge over the edge. Adam was fleetingly aware that Steckline had been thrown clear, had somehow disappeared.

Instinct had Adam leaping from the wagon, but he jumped into space, felt himself falling, desperately clawing at thin air. He hit the ground hard, throwing out his arms in a vain attempt to protect himself as the breath was slammed from his body; he was aware that he was rolling downward through the darkness at increasing speed, over and over, bushes tearing at him and

145

somewhere below him he could hear the terrified screaming of the horse and the crash of the wagon. It seemed he rolled for an eternity, rocks jabbing into him, bushes and thorns clawing at him mercilessly. His head struck something hard. He had come to rest on his back, the stars pinwheeling whitely in his blurring vision and then he lost his way as everything merged into oblivion.

10

He was aware of a redness behind his eyelids, aware of intense pain; every part of his body felt as though it had been battered to pulp. He thought he should be dead but he was certain he was not. He blinked frantically. It was still dark. He seemed to be lying amid a dense thicket of thorny brambles, but overhead, through the tangled growth, he could see the stars. He had no way of telling how long he'd been wandering through the murky world of unconsciousness. He thought he might yet die. He became aware of the laboured, pained breathing of the horse. It was some way off, yet the sound carried clearly. The beast must have fallen a good way; perhaps the wagon had come down on top of it. Now it was obviously wheezing away the last agonized moments of its life

— but then these were brought to an abrupt end. The crack of a shot sounded and the animal's breathing ceased.

Adam heard somebody thrashing about in the thicket, stumbling in the darkness — then Steckline's voice sounded: 'Ballard, I know you're in there somewhere. Come out with your hands up!'

Adam didn't move. He lay perfectly still. He doubted he could have moved had he wanted to, he was so badly hurt. But the fact was that he had no desire to move, for he knew that Steckline would gun him down at the first opportunity. He had been lucky to come to rest in the densest, darkest part of the thicket. He suspected that Steckline was bluffing. He had no idea where Adam was and probably hoped that he had been killed in the fall — but he was leaving nothing to chance. Suddenly his gun was blasting off. He must have sent a dozen shots scything through the thicket, the muzzle-flash illuminating the darkness. Any of those bullets could have ploughed into Adam's flesh; they buzzed close to him and all he could do was curl into the smallest target he could and pray the lead passed him by. His prayers must have been answered for when the fusillade ceased, he had not been hit.

He heard Steckline pacing about for what seemed a long while, then everything went quiet. The minutes slipped away and Adam tried to convince himself that his enemy had gone, possibly intent on continuing to his cabin on foot, perhaps convinced that Adam was dead.

Adam waited maybe fifteen minutes, hearing no further sound from beyond the thicket. Up through the scraggly overgrowth he could see that the sky was beginning to grow pale as dawn seeped in. He knew that Walnut Canyon was no more than a mile distant from this spot and he figured that that was where Steckline would be headed, no doubt to destroy any evidence of Altha's body. With both Altha and Adam, as he would hope, dead, he would attempt to destroy evidence that the girl had ever been at his cabin and, as town marshal, he would try to obliterate anything to indicate he'd been involved in any form of malpractice.

But Adam had other ideas.

Gritting his teeth against his agony, he forced his limbs into movement, feeling the thorns jagging into him. His knee felt as if it was smashed, but he gingerly probed the rest of his body and felt convinced that no bones were broken and that, at worst, he was the victim of bad bruising. His escape had been a miracle.

Twenty minutes of painful dragging saw him at last free of the vicious thicket, cursing and groaning every inch of the way; at last he made it on to open ground. The thorny thicket had tortured him, but its density had saved his life. He gazed up at the ridge above his head over which the wagon had fallen.

Down to his left he spotted the wreckage of the wagon, and the dead horse lying in the shafts, the blood on its head already attracting flies. His anger against Steckline drove him to ignore his pain.

It took him another twenty minutes to haul himself up the steep bank and on to the trail, his knee still hurting him, but the pain growing less intense as he got it moving. He felt it with his fingers but could feel no broken bone. By the time he was back upon the trail the morning sun had touched the distant hills, changing from a mellow softness to a brassy glare. He glanced around for Steckline but he was nowhere to be seen. His own holster was empty, and he recalled how he had drawn his gun at the time of the struggle. No doubt the weapon had been tossed aside as the wagon went over the edge. He had no time to look for it. If he was going to kill Steckline, it would have to be with his bare hands or some other weapon.

He started to hobble along the trail towards Walnut Canyon, hatred for the man who had tried to kill him mixed with anguish over the death of his sister, rendering him oblivious to his other pains. He was convinced that Steckline would have returned to his cabin while he considered what his best line of action was. He was also counting on Steckline's believing that he had been killed. His sudden appearance would give him the element of surprise. It was worrying that Steckline would no doubt be armed and he wasn't. It was impossible to know how the future would work out, The appearance of some other traveller along the trail, somebody who would offer him assistance, would have been most welcome, but at this early hour the only sign of life other than his own came from the birds, several coyotes and once a lumbering armadillo.

It seemed an age before the rugged outline of the red sandstone openings of the canyons showed ahead of him, but at last Steckline's cabin came into view, set as it was in the meadow at the mouth of Walnut Canyon. The sight of it gave him fresh energy.

Adjacent to the cabin was a barn and as he approached he tried to keep this structure in line with the cabin, concealing him. The nearer he could get before Steckline became aware of his presence, the better. Of course, there was still the chance that the marshal might be elsewhere, but the instinct that he was here grew stronger as Adam went forward, and the prospect of Steckline harming poor Altha's remains made him groan.

Still keeping the barn between him and the cabin, he heard sounds coming from the direction of the cabin — boots scraping on the veranda boards. He had lost all sense of reason beyond the frantic desire to reach his enemy, to inflict upon him the vengeance he so richly deserved.

The left side of the barn was bathed in deep, purple shadow and he eased himself along it, keeping his eyes on the cabin. There was no sight of Steckline now, but he could hear movement from within. He came around the side of the barn, and seeing its opening slipped inside for a moment's respite, to steady his pounding anger and force himself to form some line of strategy — but the fury still broiled inside him and it was difficult to think rationally.

The barn was piled high with straw and tools and other impedimenta that went with any smallholding — and then his gaze fell on a heap of branding irons stacked in the corner. He examined them and immediate recognition dawned in him. They displayed the unmistakable, crude shape of a rocking chair and his memory clicked into place. The last time he'd seen that brand had been upon the half-decomposed hide of the dead calf in the *brasada*, left as evidence to support the lynching of Cal Gausman at the point where the crime had occurred — the lynching that would have taken place had it not been for the dire need of Seth Hardeman for medical attention.

Adam grunted with satisfaction. Here was proof that Steckline had been involved with the maverickers, was no doubt one himself — and that was the reason he'd been able to afford his fine cabin.

Adam was desperate to confront Steckline, but he needed some sort of weapon. Glancing around he spotted a two-tined pitchfork leaning against the baled hay. He grabbed hold of it and steeled himself for the violence which now seemed inevitable.

With renewed energy he cast caution aside and stepped from the barn, went past the water-trough, crossed to the cabin and mounted the steps on to the veranda. He could still hear the scurry of movement and now his nostrils were assailed by the familiar smell of kerosene. Almost immediately he heard the scrape of a match and the sudden *puff* as flame was ignited. He rushed through the open doorway into the cabin's main room. It was empty, but somebody was moving about in the bedroom, the bedroom where Altha's body lay.

The crackle of flames seizing on to tinder-dry wood was now unmistakable and, with the brightness of fire showing behind him, Kirk Steckline rushed from the room, coming face to face with Adam, his jaw sagging with surprise. But he was quick to react. His hand plunged for his gun, got it clear of its holster. In the same instant Adam hurled the pitch-fork at him, the tines piercing his gun-arm, causing him to spin round in agony and drop the weapon as blood stained his shirt-sleeve. Adam was on him in a flash, flailing great blows with his fists but somehow failing to connect. Steckline had been shocked by the hurling of the pitchfork, but he seemed only superficially injured, his strength undiminished, because he screamed out: 'I'll break you in half, damn you!'

As they crashed to the floor, Adam

got his legs in a scissor-lock around his ememy's midriff, tried to roll him over, but pain shot up from his injured knee and Steckline shook him off.

The two men struggled like angry animals, wrestling and floundering, Steckline striving to get his thumbs into Adam's eyes, but Adam turned his head. Flames danced with increasing ferocity about them, leaping high, heat rising, bathing them in orange glow. Adam realized that the whole place must have been doused with kerosene, ready to ignite. Soon they would be engulfed by a raging inferno. Adam jabbed his elbow into the other man's face, feeling the hard impact of his teeth. They fought without restraint, biting, kicking, gouging, the hatred of each momentarily blinding him to the deadly peril of being burned alive.

And then, somehow, Steckline found room to swing his arm. He punched Adam on the jaw, his fist seeming as hard as a hickory-knot, setting agony stabbing up into his skull and the mists of insensibility crowding in on him. Adam was thrown back, his legs giving way, and he plunged down amid the swirling smoke and scorching heat, fighting desperately for breath.

Steckline delayed no longer. The whole cabin was ablaze; the supports were giving way; but it was a price he had to pay if he was to preserve his integrity, and he ran from the place, knowing that his clothes were scorching. He hurled himself down in the grass, rolled over and over, until he knew he would survive, then he staggered to his feet, his breath coming in great gasps, his face blackened and bruised.

He took one backward glance, grunted with satisfaction at the sight of the blazing cabin — then ran until the air became cool about him and he knew he had made good his escape. Surely no man, he told himself, not even Adam Ballard, could survive that furnace.

* * *

Steckline was wrong. Adam lay stunned upon the cabin floor, half-suffocated by the dense smoke and kerosene fumes, the pain of his jaw seeming subsidiary to the terrible scorching that embraced his body yet thankful that he no longer had Steckline to contend with. The staccato crack of explosions sounded. It was the bullets in Steckline's discarded gun succumbing to the heat.

Adam knew his clothes were aflame. He could hear the rafters of the building caving in as flames licked about them, a wooden beam, ablaze, crashed down. He knew he only had seconds to survive unless he drove himself to move. He pressed downward with his palms, feeling the searing heat in the boarded floor; somehow he forced himself up. He charged through the open door into the outside world, still engulfed in smoke, but ahead of him he saw the black hulk of the horse-trough and he dived straight into it, head first, gasping as the coolness seeped into him. He allowed his body to enjoy some semblance of recovery; then he glanced around, but the smoke was so dense that he could see nothing of Steckline. God only knew where he'd disappeared to.

Then he thought of Altha. Her body would have been incinerated in the conflagration, just as no doubt Steckline had intended, and there was nothing he could do. Her ashes would have been lost for ever, and perhaps the reasons and secrets that had tortured her, driven her to such outrageous action, would have gone with her.

With great effort he hauled himself from the cooling water of the horse-trough, immediately conscious of the heat that was emanating from the blazing cabin; there would be nothing of it left within minutes. Adam forced movement into his limbs. He had no option but to escape from this place, to find temporary sanctuary in the adjacent trees. He also had the woebegone feeling that Steckline might still be loitering around; if he got another chance to finish Adam off he would make no mistake. Even now his entire body felt battered and stinging with the scorching it had taken.

He hobbled away, moving with all the speed he could muster, anxious to get clear of this place in which he had almost died.

Yet again he had no clear idea of what he should do apart from allow fate to unfold about him, but he felt that he must get back to Kwahadi Springs. He had few friends there; most people still held him guilty for his father's death — regarded him as a convicted murderer, and his word would count for little, but he felt he had little choice, and he was certain that Kathleen would offer him some place to rest up while he decided on his future action. He wished he had a horse, but it seemed he would have to rely on his battered legs to cover the long walk to town.

Once more he gazed around, seeing how the cabin had caved in upon itself in a mass of white, smouldering ash and flame, smoke staining the sky. He satisfied himself that there was no sign of Steckline. Thankfully he appeared long gone. Then Adam started out on his long hobble towards town, his body plagued by a hundred hurts, a sickness gripping his insides, his clothes still sodden from the horse-trough.

For once fortune favoured him. A wagon came along the trail behind him — a homesteader, a stranger, on his way to town to collect supplies — and he stopped and hauled Adam up on to the seat beside him. His simple brain could make little of Adam's story, and he shook his head in bewilderment, but he provided the transport that was so desperately needed.

Kwahadi Springs was stirring into life as they entered Main Street, the stores were opening, a few early folk were on the boardwalks. Adam kept a wary eye open for Steckline. It was possible the man had acquired a horse from some neighbour and had already arrived in town, if it was his intention to come here. Adam suspected that it was, for he had a story to tell, rumours and lies to spread if he was to retain respect. With Adam dead, the task would have been much easier, but he would have an unpleasant shock when he realized that Adam had not perished — and if the two men came face to face there would be hell to pay.

Adam dismounted from the wagon, thanked his benefactor profusely and went to the only place where he could find temporary sanctuary — the home of Kathleen McCrain. When he knocked on her door she opened up, pulling a wrap about her shoulders. The sight of him caused the colour to drain from her face and she immediately ushered him inside.

'What's happened! Are you badly hurt, Adam? You look awful.'

He shook her head, tried to dispel her worst fears. 'I guess I look worse than I am,' he said.

'You've been burned,' she exclaimed,

'and you've got bruises and cuts all over you.'

'Kathleen . . . Steckline's the one we've got to fear. He wants me dead because I know too much about him. My sister Altha is dead. I think he might have killed her.'

'But how . . . why?' She looked bewildered. But then she said, 'Sit down. I'll get you some clean clothes and a bath of water. I've got some ointment too. It'll ease the pain.'

He nodded. He was weary and a little loving care was more than welcome. Within minutes, she was peeling away his shirt and bathing his chest and arms, wincing at the sight of his scratches and bruises but thankful that all seemed superficial. Her gentle hands soothed his body. Presently, she brought him a towel, allowing him to preserve his modesty as she slipped his tattered Levis off and sponged his legs, after which she applied soothing balm.

As she worked, he told her all that had happened, speaking his words as

164

calmly as possible. Even so her eyes were wide with horror at what he had experienced, shaking her head in dismay when he spoke of Altha's death.

'It was fixed to look like suicide,' he said, 'but Steckline or somebody else could easily have placed the gun beside her after killing her.'

'Oh my God!' Kathleen exclaimed. 'You've got to be so careful now. Steckline destroyed all evidence when he burned his cabin and her body. Now everything hinges on his word. And he's the marshal. Everybody'll believe what he says.'

Adam nodded in misery.

'You've got to keep out of his way, Adam,' she went on. 'He'll get you if he possibly can. Did anybody see you come here?'

'I don't think so, but the man who brought me in on his wagon is bound to talk. Word will get to Steckline, that's for sure.'

She wrung out the sponge into the bowl. Her care had brought him considerable relief, but he still ached all over and his skin was tingling from the scorching it had taken. She stepped away from him, went to the window and gazed out. 'Everything's normal,' she said.

'Kathleen,' he said earnestly, 'if Steckline doesn't come looking for me, I've got to find him. He can't get away with whatever crimes he's committed. He knows more about Altha's death than he's let on, and also I found evidence that he'd been marvericking. Probably involved with the Gausmans.'

She didn't say anything, just looked downright miserable. They both lapsed into silence, bound up with their own thoughts, then at last she said: 'He'll kill you, Adam, then lie through his teeth to clear his name.'

'He won't kill me if I see him first,' Adam countered. 'Kathleen, I've got a favour to ask.'

'Anythin',' she responded.

'I've got to protect myself. I lost my gun when I fell from that wagon. Can I borrow your father's gun?'

She hesitated, fearing that if he was armed it would place him in greater danger — but then she realized he was right. He had to protect himself. She disappeared into another room and a moment later returned with her father's revolver and gunbelt. 'He'd want you to have it,' she murmured as she handed it to him.

11

She insisted that he must rest. Her father's bedroom had remained as if he still used it and for the rest of the day Adam slept intermittently. Although his instincts wanted nothing more than to be with Kathleen, for he loved her nearness, he knew it would be unwise to remain in her house any longer than necessary because he felt he was placing her in danger, but she was very insistent. However, come evening of that day matters were taken out of their hands for there came a heavy knocking on the door and through the curtain she saw four of Steckline's associates.

'I guess he's sworn them in as deputies,' Kathleen whispered.

Adam was on his feet instantly, strapping on the former lawman's gunbelt. He felt restricted in Amos's clothing, for Kathleen's father had been somewhat smaller than he. However his own clothes were beyond redemption being torn, bloodstained and scorched, so he was glad enough to have something to wear.

'They may try to burst in,' he gasped. 'You'll be in danger.'

The hammering on the door had been renewed.

'I can handle them, don't worry,' she said. 'You best get out the back way. Let's just pray they haven't got the house surrounded. Maybe you should hide out in the *brasada* for the time being.'

She pressed some money into his hand. 'Pay me back later.'

He nodded, seeing sense in what she said, realizing that every moment he delayed the greater peril she was in. He rushed through the kitchen and opened the back door. All appeared clear so he gave her arm a quick squeeze and murmured, 'Thanks for everythin', Kathleen.' Then he took to his heels.

Glancing back, he saw no sign of

pursuit. He ran across some scrub ground and re-entered the town, changing his pace to a brisk walk and keeping to narrow alleyways. He passed several people but they didn't spare him a glance and moments later he reached the livery-stable. As he entered the hostler gave him an alarmed stare.

'The law's after you!' he cried. He held out a Wanted poster. *Adam Ballard . . . wanted for murder and arson . . . Dead or alive.*

'Saddle my horse quick,' Adam said.

The man hesitated, but Adam slipped his gun from its holster and waved it in the air. 'All right . . . all right!' the man said. He led Adam's bay horse from its stall and cinched on the saddle while Adam slipped the bridle into place. He gave the man what he owed him, then mounted up and heeled the animal from the barn. A minute later he was riding out of town.

Meanwhile Kathleen had opened her door to the four deputies. 'There's no need to knock the door down,' she complained.

'We've been sworn in as deputies.' It was the bullnecked Sam Pitts who spoke, his tone belligerent. 'We're after Adam Ballard. He killed his sister, burned Kirk Steckline's place down! We've got reason to believe you're hidin' him.'

Three other men, Will Steelman, Sam Crossman and Ed Catrum were crowding behind him. They had all previously been cronies of the Gausmans. Now they were clearly anxious to push their way into the house and search for Adam, but Kathleen stood her ground, blocking the doorway. In her firmest voice she said: 'He's not here!' She chose her words carefully to avoid lying.

The severity of her tone took them aback.

They hesitated, then Sam Pitts said: 'Well, the skunk's in this town somewhere and we intend to find him.' They backed off, muttering, and left her.

Adam rode straight for the Double-X. He had to let his stepmother know the awful news of Altha's death. He also had to let her know the true version of events, although whether she would believe him was another matter. But when he reached the ranch, he was greeted with her customary coldness. She already knew the grim news. One of Steckline's men had come looking for Adam and told her what had happened.

'How could you do it?' she screamed at Adam. 'Killed your father . . . and now you've killed your sister! You're a murderer, a cold-blooded murderer, Adam Ballard, and I hope you hang for what you've done.'

For a moment he thought she was going to attack him, to beat him to death with her scrawny fists, but at that moment a frail-looking Seth Hardeman appeared in the doorway behind her. He was pointing a gun at Adam.

'Get away from here,' he snarled. 'We don't want you here. Get away and never come back!'

Adam hesitated, started to speak but then realized how futile it would be. They would believe nothing that he said. He turned on his heel, mounted his horse and left the ranch. He could do nothing else but take Kathleen's advice and hide out in the *brasada* until he could form a plan for his future. The whole world looked overwhelmingly bleak to him at that moment.

Kirk Steckline had obviously spread the word in town that Adam had murdered his sister, though for what motive he couldn't imagine — and that he had burned Steckline's cabin to the ground to destroy the evidence, but Adam's arrival had ruined his plans. He'd acted quickly in getting the wanted dodgers issued. And there was no doubt about it. The people of Kwahadi Springs would swallow his story without question.

But Adam swore to himself that he

would fight to clear his name. A skunk like Steckline could not be allowed to get away with his crimes.

However, there was something of which Adam was unaware. As soon as he had left the livery, the hostler had wasted little time in rushing over to the marshal's office. Steckline had been absent, out searching the town, but his newly sworn-in deputy Ed Catrum left a hasty note for his boss and then set out to follow Adam's trail. When Steckline returned from his searching, he rapidly summoned his remaining deputies and left town on the same trail. He wanted Adam dead, and the sooner he silenced him the more secure he would feel.

★　★　★

The most obvious place that Adam Ballard was likely to head for appeared to be the Double-X ranch, and sure enough Steckline and his three deputies found Catrum on the ridge that overlooked the spread. He was able to confirm that their quarry had arrived there about twenty minutes earlier. His bay horse stood hitched to the rail outside the main house. Steckline grunted with impatience. He could hardly go storming into the ranch house and gun Adam down, much as the prospect appealed to him. He had no desire to arrest him, for that would mean formally charging him with murder and putting him on trial, with the circuit judge in attendance. That would make matters far more complicated because questions would be asked and the last thing Steckline wanted was an in-depth investigation of events.

Evening was now slipping in and it would be disastrous for Steckline if Adam escaped under the cover of darkness. Of course there was the possibility that Adam intended to stay at the ranch overnight, although the fact that he had not stabled his horse indicated that his intention was only for a brief stay.

In the event, Steckline and his posse did not have long to wait. Adam remained in the house for little more than twenty minutes. Steckline made sure his posse stayed hidden as Adam left the house, mounted his animal and left the spread, heading towards the *brasada*.

Steckline felt excited now, for he felt pretty sure he could catch his man. 'Let's go get him!' he cried, and he urged his party in pursuit. It would be easy to explain that Adam had resisted the attempt to arrest him — and that in the quick flurry of shots that followed, he had been killed. After all, Steckline had made certain that the wanted dodger had specified 'dead or alive'. But the light was fading fast and so haste was important.

Five minutes later Adam became aware of the thunder of hoofs behind him, and glancing back it took little imagination to realize that Steckline and his posse were coming after him. He heeled his bay horse for greater speed and ahead he saw the dark fringe of the thicket. If he could reach that ahead of his pursuers, he might stand a chance of escape. But he noted that the posse were all mounted on fleet mustangs, ideal for moving through the dense *brasada*, whereas his bay horse was a big cumbersome mount — good for the open range, but lacking the sure-footedness best suited for moving through mesquite brush.

However, he was soon entering the gloomy thickets, forcing his way through thorn and tangled undergrowth. He was ever-conscious that his enemies were closing on him. There were five of them and if it came to a stand-off fight, his chances would not be good.

And then disaster struck. The bay horse stepped into a gopher-hole, stumbled and went down, throwing Adam from his saddle. He rolled into the undergrowth, feeling thorns spike into his body. He scrambled up, looked around for his mount, but it had moved on, lumbering away, its leg hurt, and with dismay Adam realized that he could rely on it no more. He spotted a fallen tree-trunk and threw himself down behind it, drawing his gun. There was one thing that offered him an advantage, and that was the encroaching gloom of night.

The pound and rustle of his pursuers was suddenly very close as they combed through the mesquite. They knew well enough that he had fallen and probably reckoned he would be easy to catch. A shot blasted off, passing close enough to warn him that they had a fair idea of his position. He held his own fire, knowing that once he opened up they would be able to pin-point exactly where he was.

One horseman passed so close that he could almost have touched him, but then moved on like a grey shadow. The others were all around, thrashing about in the undergrowth, calling to each other. Then Steckline's voice sounded: 'Come out with you hands up, Ballard, otherwise we're coming in and we'll gun you down!'

Adam crouched as low as he could, nigh shrinking into the spongy earth. He knew that the instant he showed himself he would be riddled with lead. There was a moment of silence, then he heard their voices, though the exact words were indistinguishable.

Suddenly Steckline shouted: 'Right! Let him have it!' and the air was all at once alive with bullets, splintering the wood of his cover and the bark of surrounding trees. The orange glow of gunfire illuminated the gloom. Adam felt something smack into his back; for a moment thought he had been shot, but then discovered it was merely a chunk of splintered bark. But lead whizzed around him, he knew that his luck could not last for ever, and he was conscious of the fact that his enemies were closing in about him in a tightening ring.

A voice that seemed but a few yards from him cried out: 'Dawgone it!

179

Careful where you're damn well shootin'. You winged me!'

The shooting petered out. Somebody else called: 'Where is the bastard!'

Adam edged to his left, moving slowly so as to make no sound. The darkness was now total, what little light there was stifled out by the overhanging branches. He guessed that he must have somehow passed through the ring that his enemies had formed about him, and he heard the nervous snuffle of their mustangs which they'd left when they'd closed in to finish him off. He decided he had to take a desperate chance. He rose to his feet and burst through the thicket to where the animals were grouped. Moving rapidly he grabbed the bridle of the nearest animal and swung into the saddle. Simultaneously, he fired his revolver into the air, its sudden roar panicking the mustangs into flight. They scattered through the mesquite in a flash, and he, astride one animal, went with them.

Behind him he heard the vicious

cursing of his pursuers, but now he heeled his mustang for all-out speed. He crashed through the undergrowth and was away, the thorns and branches tearing at him, but he did not care. A few desultory shots snapped in his wake, but his enemies were firing blind and the lead whined off into thin air.

His nimble mount darted through the mesquite with amazing agility — and he knew that, with darkness on his side, his enemies stranded on foot and the vast *brasada* stretching before him, he could make good his immediate escape.

*   *   *

The gloom of night descended about him, and with it the ghostly cries of coyotes, owls and other nocturnal creatures. After a while, Adam slowed his pace, allowed the game little mustang to pick its own way. Nothing seemed to matter as long as he increased the distance between himself and Steckline's thugs. Presently he trailed to a halt. The mustang was weary and needed a rest, and so did he. He also needed time to think. His immediate escape was merely a stepping-stone. He had to form some strategy for the future, and one thing was worrying him more and more. Kathleen was in a highly vulnerable position, for it might be discovered that she had befriended him. There was little doubt that although Steckline's immediate attempt to kill him had failed, he would not give up. He could not afford to if he was to establish himself as town marshal of Kwahadi Springs. Furthermore, Kathleen might well find herself in trouble for aiding and abetting a supposed criminal. He needed to do something to protect her — but what? If he showed up in town again he was on a one-way ticket to the next world. And yet did he have any option?

He could travel through the *brasada*, head further and further north, maybe towards Montana and Wyoming, maybe disappear under an assumed name and find employment as a cowhand or some other job where his identity would not be questioned. But that would be the coward's way out out. He had left jail intent on proving that he had been wrongly sentenced. The fact that his efforts had somehow landed him in far deeper trouble than he had ever anticipated almost seemed incidental. Steckline was a mavericker, a cohort of evil men like the Gausmans. He could not be allowed to get away with it. And there was only one person who had an inkling of the truth — and that was Adam himself. Furthermore, there was Kathleen to be considered, and Adam now knew that he loved her more than anybody else in the entire world. He would not turn his back on her.

He bedded down that night in the dank obscurity of the *brasada*, having hobbled the mustang. The beast had served him well and whatever tomorrow brought, he would need the animal. As for his own bay horse, he hoped its injury had not been serious and that it would ultimately find its way back to the Double-X. His riderless return would raise all sorts of questions. Steckline might even claim that their mission had been a success and that Adam was lying dead, maybe consumed by wolves, in the far reaches of the big thicket. Provided Adam did not reappear, his ends might be served. His word would not be questioned and he would retain his respectable image and, when he chose, extend his criminal activities.

But as Adam lapsed into uneasy sleep, glad enough of the horse blanket and the saddle for his bedding, he was growing more and more determined. He would neither turn his back on Steckline — nor desert the only real friend he had in the world, Kathleen McCrain. Tomorrow he would return to town and face down his enemies, though he hoped that he might awaken with an exact course of action clearer in his mind.

12

He was awake long before the first glimmering of light had filtered down through the overhead tangle of branches, but already the wilderness was alive with the scurryings of nature. He was hungry and to his delight he found some bread and sowbelly in the saddle-bag of the mustang, to which he did full justice. Sleep had brought no clear solution to his problems — but of one thing he had become increasingly sure. The future for him did not lie in flight to a distant and obscure place where he would forever be looking over his shoulder in anticipation of being trailed by some representative of the law.

With a heavy heart, and with no clear idea of what he could hope to achieve, he turned the mustang back towards Kwahadi Springs. If he was forced to, he would gun Steckline down himself and face the consequences.

The town was drowsing in its normal noon torpidity as he rode up Main Street. Of the few people who walked the sideboards, none spared him a glance. He passed Kathleen's house, satisfying himself that all appeared in order. He yearned to call on her, but decided against implicating her further in his troubles. He kept a wary eye open for Steckline or any of his men. He saw no sign of them, but was ever conscious that a single shot from a shadowed doorway could put an end to any plans he might have.

He had made up his mind. A person who might offer him some hope of proving his innocence was the town mayor — Edward Shermer. He did not know the man, having never met him, but he had heard that he had a reputation as an honest and hard-working individual who had the interests of the town very much at heart. He also happened to be the local bank-manager. Right now, the bank would be closed as was customary at midday, and Adam was counting on finding the man at his home on the outskirts of town.

He rode the streets constantly on the look-out for his enemies, but he found the mayor's home without being molested. It was an elegant house as befitted the man's position, built of freshly painted white timber with neatly curtained windows and a broad veranda upon which were a number of rocking-chairs. He knocked on the door and after a moment a matronly-looking woman opened up who he guessed was Mrs Shermer. She looked at him with a puzzled expression as if his face was familiar but she couldn't quite place it.

'The mayor,' he said. 'I'd very much like a word with him. Is he at home?'

'Yes. Who shall I say . . . ?'

'Adam Ballard.'

Her face paled a little, but she nodded and turned back into the house. A moment later he was confronted by a tall, scrawny-thin, white-bearded man with nervous weasel eyes, who looked as if he had stepped straight out of the Bible. 'I understand you're in some sort of trouble, Mr Ballard,' he announced.

Adam nodded. 'I believe that Kirk Steckline will kill me if he gets the opportunity. I need to talk to you. Some place where my back is covered.'

'I understand. You must come in, but first may I ask you to remove your gun.'

Adam hesitated, not absolutely sure that he could trust this man. He might well be placing himself in a trap, but it was a chance he decided to take, so he unstrapped his gunbelt and handed it to the mayor who said, 'Come inside.'

He followed Shermer inside and shortly found himself seated in the parlour. Mrs Shermer brought a jug of lemonade and some glasses on a tray and Shermer poured out the drinks.

'Why have you come here?' he asked.

'You are a wanted man. The marshal has issued a warrant for your arrest.'

'I know,' Adam said. 'But there is so much more to the story than he makes out. As you are aware, my sister was kidnapped by Cornelius Gausman and I searched everywhere to try and find her. I trailed Gausman to Waco, to the home of his sister-in-law. I eventually tracked him down to a saloon. He drew a gun on me, shot at me, but his shot was off-target.'

Adam removed his hat and displayed the bullet hole in the brim. 'That's how close his shot went. He was about to fire again, but I drew my own gun and I gunned him down. The town marshal of Waco agreed I had no option. It was self-defence. The upsetting thing was that I still had no information about the whereabouts of my sister. Anyway, I came back to Kwahadi Springs and felt it was my duty to inform the marshal of events. However he wasn't at his office, so I decided to ride out to his place in the hope that he was there.'

Shermer was listening, nodding understandingly.

'When I got there I made a terrible discovery. I found my sister's body.' He hesitated as the memory of it choked him. After a moment he continued: 'She had been shot in the head, whether by her own hand or somebody else's wasn't obvious.'

Shermer gave Adam a comforting pat on the shoulder. 'A terrible shock for you,' he sympathized.

Adam took a gulp of cooling lemonade. 'I reckoned the best thing I could do was to head back to town and confront Steckline — find out what Altha was doing at his place and what had happened to her. This time I found him in his office and he seemed shocked at the news I gave him. He suggested that we take a wagon out to his cabin and bring the body back to the undertaker in town and I agreed. But on the way he drew his gun on me.

I grabbed his arm and we had a fight. The wagon went over the edge of the trail and fell into a ravine. He jumped clear, but I fell into the undergrowth. It was dark by that time. He fired several shots at me; he didn't hit me — but I guess he thought he'd killed me.'

Adam went on with the rest of the story, saying how he had found the branding-irons in the barn and then discovered that Steckline was setting his cabin, and Altha's body, ablaze. He also explained how he had been chased into the *brasada* by Steckline and his men, but had escaped them — and how he had eventually decided to turn to the mayor for help.

'You tell a fantastic story,' Shermer said. He pondered for a long moment, then he stood up. 'Stay where you are for a moment. There are some papers I need to check.'

He moved across to a desk in the corner of the room, opened a drawer and reached inside. When his hand emerged he was holding a gun which he aimed at Adam. His expression had changed from one of compassionate understanding to one of extreme meanness.

'You're a wanted man,' he said. 'You've probably told me a pack of lies, but that will be for the judge to decide. As far as I'm concerned, Kirk Steckline has done a good job since he's been in office. I've got no reason to disbelieve his story. I'm locking you up in the town jail until Judge Ramsburg can get here. He won't take kindly to being dragged back here so soon, but he'll make judgement. Now raise your hands, or it will be me who does the next shooting!'

Adam was aghast. He realized he'd made the gravest mistake in coming here, in trusting this man. With the gun levelled firmly at him, he had no option but to do as he was told.

★ ★ ★

The town jail was a small block with two interior cells. Its floor was flagstone and its walls were thick stone. It was primarily designed for the accommodation of overnight drunks, but was sometimes used for more important tasks. On such occasions the drunks were turfed out and returned to the streets. Sanitary pails were emptied infrequently, the treatment of lime and whitewash doing little to alleviate the stench. The prisoner, securely manacled, was marched across the street twice a day to a wash-house for ablutions. The jail, situated at the eastern end of town, came under the jurisdiction of the mayor who provided guards when necessary. With Adam incarcerated, two armed guards took up position outside, the county sheriff was informed of events and arrangements made for the attendance of the circuit judge at the earliest opportunity.

The daytime heat in the cell was little short of intolerable, for the only ventilation, apart from the barred door, came from a window near to the ceiling. This opened on to the street and Adam was in constant fear that somebody who wished him harm might poke a gun through and shoot him. In consequence, he spent most of the nights sleeping on the floor with his blankets lying crumpled on the bunk to imply his presence. He could well imagine Steckline's desire to avoid the case going to trial increasing every day, even though he was in a strong position to gain a guilty verdict for the prisoner.

Adam sweated away the hours and days in misery, his only pleasure being the daily visits of Kathleen McCrain. She brought him baskets of provisions and other things to make his stay as comfortable as was humanly possible. But she told him some grim news. It was common knowledge that she had helped him escape the law, for his presence in her house had been observed by a neighbour. Very little could happen within the town community without all and sundry becoming aware. In consequence she had been warned that she faced charges of aiding and abetting a criminal and told that on no account was she to leave town.

'I'm real sorry that you're implicated in this, Kathleen,' Adam said.

She laughed dismissively. 'All will be sorted out when the judge arrives, don't worry. Steckline's case won't stand up.'

Adam wasn't so sure, but he tried to put on a brave face for this girl he loved. The truth was that he felt his own case was as thin as rice paper, and there appeared to be no subtlety in the way Judge Ramsburg reached his conclusions.

On the fourth day of his confinement Adam had another visitor — a young attorney who had been supplied by the county, called Chris Benjamin. He wore a black broadcloth coat and striped waistcoat. He appeared a bright young man, skinny as a beanpole, yet smart in his business suit. He possessed a deep, strong voice and a cheerful disposition, and he sat with Adam for several hours meticulously taking notes and detailing Adam's version of events. He neither expressed belief nor disbelief in what he recorded, but Adam had little doubt that the man would do his best for him.

Meanwhile, he saw nothing of Steckline or his cohorts. He wondered what plots the marshal was forming. One thing was certain. He would not be idle in preparing for the trial.

After Christopher Benjamin, the defence attorney, had taken all the notes he required, his visits ceased. Adam missed him, for he was a pleasant young man. Kathleen brought a chess-board and pieces into the cell and they sat for some hours playing the game. She was surprisingly astute at it, far more so than Adam, but they played with great humour and she claimed that as she was facing charges she should be retained in the cell next to Adam's. The mayor thought otherwise and she was kept under town arrest. But her spirits remained buoyant and she was a great comfort to Adam. As for his stepmother and Seth Hardeman, he heard nothing, but he guessed they would be watching events with interest, no doubt believing that he deserved everything that was likely to come his way.

Adam did not trust his guards, for they were a lazy crowd, and would just as likely fall asleep when on duty as not. Any stealthy assassin could approach the jail during the night hours and fire in through the bars of the window.

But gradually time dragged away until at last Judge Ramsburg arrived in town and Adam learned that the trial was to start on the next day.

Adam endured a sleepless night. Come the following morning he was taken over to the wash-house where he had a thorough hose-down and shave. After this he was given a clean set of clothing and offered a breakfast, though his appetite was lacking. The truth was he felt downright sick.

When he was led in, the courtroom was packed to capacity, the atmosphere stifling with the rising warmth of that summer's day. For one moment Adam's glance met the hard eyes of his stepmother, sitting near the back.

Alongside her was Seth Hardeman, looking frail and just a shadow of his old self. But obviously he had made progress and was well enough to attend the trial.

Judge Ramsburg occupied his customary place, sitting behind his huge maple desk on a raised platform above the well of the court, looking imperious as he peered down from beneath his great eyebrows as owl-like as ever.

Adam, still manacled, sat between his attorney and Kathleen, who periodically rested a comforting hand upon his. She wore a mauve dress and long white gloves. Her hair was tied in a tight knot beneath a prim bonnet. She knew that today she was not on trial for 'aiding and abetting'. Her trial would come later, but she showed no concern about this, retaining her belief that Adam would be found innocent.

It seemed to take an eternity for the jury to be sworn in, the judge showing increasing impatience by constantly glancing at his pocket-watch. Each attorney asked the same sequence of questions and rejected one citizen after the another on some technicality until eventually satisfaction was reached and the all-male panel, residents of the area, took its place in the appointed box. None was known to Adam.

At last the judge sighed with considerable relief. 'I am satisfied that you are all aware of your duties and when the time comes to render your verdict you will act with conscience and courage and prove that in this state of Texas no man can consider himself above the law. The sole purpose of this court is to establish a certainty of punishment for the guilty and a rigid protection for the innocent. Criminals must know that they will pay with their own life if they have committed murder.'

Now Adam was made to stand and the judge read out the indictment. 'Are you Adam Ballard?'

'I am, your honour.'

'Then there are two charges against

you. The first is that you murdered your sister, Altha Ballard, by shooting her in the head. And the second is that you destroyed evidence by burning down the cabin of Marshal Kirk Steckline. Do you plead guilty or not guilty?'

'Not guilty.'

13

At this point, the prosecuting attorney, Albert Gibbon, got up from his assigned table and took the stand. He had a hound-dog face, loose-skinned and pliable, and he made use of his every expression to express disgust, shock and horror at the words he spoke. He reminded the court of Adam's previous conviction for murder, of his rebellious youth when he had often shown his quick temper. He spoke of how the family had always been subject to domestic strife which had sometimes turned to violent altercation. Such, he maintained, lay behind the compulsion that had led to Adam Ballard killing his sister — just as he had done his father.

'I submit, gentlemen of the jury,' he proclaimed, 'that just as Adam Ballard provoked the shameful incident in which he shot down his honest father, he just as brutally slew his innocent sister. The period he spent behind bars only increased his grudge against the world. But no doubt he was glad enough to cower behind bars while his contemporaries fought for their beliefs in the War Between the States on the battlefields of Shiloh and Bull Run. He further demonstrated his ability to kill by gunning down Cornelius Gausman in Waco.'

At this point the defence attorney Christopher Benjamin jumped to his feet with a strong objection, claiming that the Gausman killing was in selfdefence, which the judge supported, instructing Gibbons to stick to relevant matter rather than conjecture.

Even so the prosecutor rambled on for an entire hour, painting Adam's character blacker and blacker.

After his conclusion the first prosecution witness was called — none other than Marshal Kirk Steckline himself. This was the first time Adam had seen him since their fight in the blazing cabin. Steckline, looking truculent and smug and wearing a smart necktie, avoided Adam's eye, took his place on the stand and was sworn in. Soon he was relating his version of events in a confident voice, prompted by the prosecuting attorney. Adam was sorely tempted to shout out that much of what those present were hearing was a pack of lies, but, cautioned by his attorney's grip on his arm, he restrained himself and remained silent.

Steckline told how Altha had arrived at his cabin in the middle of one night and pleaded with him to take her in, saying that Gausman had let her go. He admitted that he and Altha had had an affair and that she claimed that she was carrying his child, though he doubted this. She stated that under such circumstances she was afraid to go home and wanted her presence kept secret. Feeling sorry for her, and in view of their previous relationship, he had given her shelter as any compassionate person would have done to help a young lady in such distress.

But one evening when he had gone home, he had discovered that Altha had been shot dead and that Adam Ballard was attempting to set fire to his cabin; he assumed this was to destroy evidence of the fact that Ballard had murdered his sister. Ballard had attacked him, tried to kill him, but he had overcome him and had managed to get out of the blazing cabin, only just escaping with his life. At the time he had imagined that Ballard had been killed in the fire. But this had not been so. Ballard had subsequently returned to town, been sheltered by Miss McCrain, and then attempted to escape from the posse that had been set up to effect his capture. The posse had trailed him into the *brasada* where once again fortune had favoured him. He had stolen one of the posse's mustangs and escaped. The next thing that he,

Steckline, had heard of him was after the mayor had arrested him and placed him in the town prison.

Christopher Benjamin, Adam's defence lawyer, cross-examined him, but his story appeared rocksolid and when he stepped down from the stand Adam could feel a tide of hatred rising against him through the courtroom. Benjamin's face appeared flushed and disconcerted. Other witnesses were called; they were the members of Steckline's posse, all of whom substantiated what the marshal had already said and spoke of the high regard he was earning as marshal of the town.

Adam was next called and he told his story in exactly the same form as he had related it to the mayor.

The prosecutor, still fresh from having obtained the conviction of Cal Gausman, attempted to tear Adam's evidence to shreds. Since the prosecutor was a past master at this, Adam returned to his seat feeling shaken and discredited.

At four o'clock Judge Ramsburg

adjourned proceedings for the day, warning the members of the jury not to discuss the case with anybody. Adam rose, felt the warm lips of Kathleen touch his cheek, and was returned to his cell, there to spend a restless night cast adrift in a sea of loneliness.

Next morning, a crowd of men and women awaited outside the courthouse as the county clerk arrived to unlock the door. Within seconds of the court being reconvened, every seat in the room was occupied, and many people were obliged to remain standing.

Shortly, both attorneys were conducting their summaries. The outcome seemed to rest on who was to be believed. It was the town marshal's word against that of a man who had already served time for murder. Adam had raised the point that he had seen the maverickers' branding-irons in Steckline's barn. Apparently Benjamin Christopher had carried out a search, but the evidence had been removed and there was no trace of them.

Adam was aware that the case was flowing against him. Steckline was looking well pleased with himself.

Judge Ramsburg spoke in a slow and deliberate voice, loading his words heavily in support of Adam's guilt. Eventually, in the middle of the afternoon, the jury retired to consider its verdict. Adam was returned to his cell across the street, and sat with his head in his hands, having little hope.

At last he was summoned back to the courtroom which was once again overflowing as the judge made his entrance. The jury filed back into the courtroom, and the judge enquired if the verdict had been reached.

'It has, Your Honour.' The foreman of the jury handed his paper up to the judge. Having read this Ramsburg asked Adam to stand, and when he did so he went through his customary wordage.

'Adam Ballard, you have been charged on two counts. The first is the murder of your sister Altha Ballard and the second is that you attempted, indeed succeeded, in destroying the evidence of your crimes. You have had a fair trial and the jury has unanimously found you guilty of both charges.' He paused, drummed his fingers on the table several times, then continued: 'I do not make the law of this society. It has been duly legislated by democratic process. There is but one sentence for these crimes, and I have no right to change it. Before I pronounce this sentence have you anything to say?'

Adam felt dismay seeping into every part of his body. 'I am innocent,' he said. But a murmur of disbelief rippled through the court.

The judge had assumed the same dour expression that had been on his owlish face when he had sentenced Cal Gausman to death. He cleared his throat, clearly a man who enjoyed having the power of life and death over other human beings.

Suddenly a voice shouted from the back of the court room. 'Hold on!'

The judge paused as he was about to

make further utterances. All eyes swivelled to the rear of the court. A man had walked in through the open doorway. He was a portly Mexican in a wide sombrero. A goatee decorated his chin in the fashion of a *conquistador*. His jacket and chivarras were embellished with heavy side-buckles. He was waving a paper in his hand. 'You must read this!' he cried in a thick accent.

The judge was bristling with indignation, his face flushed. 'Sir, you have no right to interrupt a court of law.'

The Mexican was not deterred. 'What I have here ees important.' He waved his paper again. 'My daughter ees Lucinda Cabellero. She was Steckline's housekeeper. It was she who discovered the woman's body. Beside it she found this note.'

A murmur of speculation cut through the room.

'It was also my daughter who shot at Adam Ballard and tried to frighten him away,' Señor Cabellero added when the hush returned.

The Mexican pushed his way forward, people moving aside to make way. He walked right up to the judge and placed his paper on the table before him. Judge Ramsburg was scowling, his expression angry. He was not used to having his sessions interrupted in this way, but grudgingly he picked up the paper and scanned what it said. The courtroom had gone silent; everybody was shocked by this event.

It seemed that an age passed while Ramsburg read. His hands were shaking. At last he raised his gaze from the paper, cleared his throat almost nervously, then he said, 'I think it is important that the court hears what is written on this paper. It is a note, indeed a letter, written by Altha Ballard, the sister of the accused.'

A burble of further expectation filled the courtroom. The judge was about to bang his gravel but an overwhelming demand for hush came from so many lips that the gathering quieted.

'This letter was intended to be read

by the step-mother of the deceased girl.' The judge shot a withering glance at the Mexican who stood unflinchingly before him. 'May I ask where you got this letter from, sir?'

'Altha Ballard asked my daughter to take it to her stepmother,' the Mexican responded, 'but Lucia did not do so because she feared it would get Señor Steckline into trouble. She could not read it. She does not read English. She did not want to give it to me, but I found it in her possession and considered, in fairness to justice, that it should be brought here today and that it should be read out to the court.'

'Yes . . . yes,' the judge blustered. He did not like being told what to do. 'I will read it now.' He again cleared his throat, then he started to read. 'My dear mother, for eight years my life has been a living nightmare of guilt. As you know, my hair has turned white and I am but a shadow of my old self. Without the Bible I would have been completely lost, but now life means nothing to me. I cannot face it. I cannot live with this terrible deceit any longer.

'Just over eight years ago I was deeply in love with Jimmy Caldwell. I know we were young, scarcely more than children, but that did not seem to matter. What was important was that we intended to marry just as soon as we could. Pa knew how we felt about each other, but he despised the Caldwell family over some business deal which had happened in the past, and he resented that Jimmy and I loved each other, One day in the barn at home he caught Jimmy and me kissing and he flew into a rage, shouting and waving his fists like a crazy man. He was real mad, and in his anger he shot Adam's dog and and after that he and Adam went at each other — and they were still rowing as they set out for the *brasada*. I felt absolutely humiliated. I wanted to hurt Father in some way, to punish him for what he had done to Jimmy and me. So I took a pistol and followed them. They never saw me nor realized I was there. I was trembling with anger. I had never felt like that before. When they stopped to rest their horses, I raised the pistol and pointed in their direction. To this day, I swear I never meant to hit Father. I just intended to scare him. But my hands were shaking so much and the gun went off, and the next thing I knew was that Father was lying on the ground, his head covered in blood.'

A ripple of amazement went round the court room. Folks could hardly believe what they were hearing, and after a moment the judge restored silence by hammering with his gravel. Then he read on.

'I was really afraid. I turned my horse, was about to gallop off, but another shot cracked out. It was Adam who had fired at me, although I am sure he did not realize who I was. I felt fire scorch along my ribs, fell from the horse and knew that blood was pouring from me. I managed to get back on the horse and spur him away.

'To this day, nobody knows that it was me who killed our father. I knew that Adam was arrested, charged with the murder. But I allowed him to face trial and be sentenced. All I can say is that, had he been sentenced to death, I would have owned up. But I was too cowardly to confess at the time, and nobody believed him when he said he was innocent. I let him serve eight years in prison for a crime he did not commit. I have lived in a hell of guilt, and I wish that I could have made it up to him in some way, but there was no way I could make amends.

'And everything was made worse by what happened after he was released from prison, having undergone a punishment he in no way deserved. Over and over, I have prayed to God for forgiveness. And then, after Seth Hardeman's fight with the maverickers in the *brasada*, I was kidnapped by Cornelius Gausman and when his twin brother was hanged I thought he would kill me but I did not care for myself, only for the little one inside me. You see, I had fallen in love with Kirk Steckline, because I thought he was a good man and would marry me, especially when he learned he was to be a father. But now I have decided that I cannot live any longer. My baby does not deserve to die, but he would deserve a better mother than I would ever make. In consequence I have decided that we shall go together, and I pray that in the next world God will find it in his heart to forgive me. Words cannot express how sorry I am for the terrible thing I did. Your stepdaughter, Altha.'

As the judge finished reading, the courtroom was a buzz of uproar. Despite being manacled, Adam came to his feet, stumbled forward and embraced the surprised Mexican, this man whom he had never met before and yet this day had saved his life. A man of honour to whom he would forever be grateful.

Once again the judge was hammering away with his gavel, somehow bringing the court to order.

But it was not his voice that came next. Dr Wilbur Fischer had come to his feet.

'Eight years ago,' he cried out, 'Altha Ballard came to me and asked for confidential medical treatment. She asked me to promise never to say that I had treated her. She was not the first young lady to come to me with such a request, and I immediately suspected that she was pregnant. I promised her I would say nothing.'

The judge's mouth was sagging slightly as the doctor continued:

'But to my surprise, she was not with child. What she needed was treatment of a bullet scrape along her ribs. I asked her how she got this, but she was so upset and she would not tell me. I cleaned the wound and bandaged it up and told her to rest. She told me that she would stay with Jimmy Caldwell until she was fit enough to go home.

Before she left me, she again requested that I told nobody about it. Next day, I had to leave for Austin on business. I was away for almost a month, so I was unaware of events back here, unaware that Adam Ballard had been charged with the murder of his father and sentenced to prison. I gave little thought to the matter thereafter. In fact it is only in view of this letter that I now recall the event. But I have honoured my word of medical confidentiality. However now that Altha is no more, and has in fact revealed that terrible secret which she lived with all those years, I do not believe that she would mind me speaking out about what happened.'

He paused for a moment to recover his breath. He was not used to speaking at such length.

'It now appears obvious to me,' he went on, 'that it was her brother who inadvertently shot her after their father had died. He did not smear his father's blood on the mesquite as misleading

217

evidence, as the court implied. It was his sister's blood. I believe it proves that Adam Ballard was an innocent man and I regret deeply that I was unable to prevent his serving all those years in prison. I know that Adam tried to move heaven and earth in his efforts to find Altha after she was kidnapped. He loved her and I believe he would have served the eight years in prison willingly if it avoided her having to do so. That is all I have to say.' And he sat down, removed his glasses and started to polish them with a large handkerchief.

For a long minute, it seemed that Judge Ramsburg was at a complete loss for words. He tugged on his swallow-tailed beard with nervous fingers. In all his experience, he had never encountered any case like this one — a case in which he had come so close to administering a blatantly wrong judgment.

At last he found his voice — a strangely humble voice. 'Under the circumstances which have today come to light, I feel I have no option but to quash the findings of this case and acquit Adam Ballard of the charges. It seems to me that it should not be Ballard standing in the dock today, but Kirk Steckline, who is in no way worthy of the appointment as town marshal of Kwahadi Springs. In fact he has been guilty of the most heinous crime of trying to divert the true cause of justice and I have little doubt that Adam Ballard spoke the truth when he stated that he saw the branding-irons of maverickers in Steckline's barn. I believe Steckline welcomed the opportunity to use his position as marshal as a front for criminal activities.'

'It's all a damned lie!' It was Steckline's scream sounding from the rear of the courtroom.

'Do not blaspheme in court!' the judge thundered. But Steckline was not listening because all eyes had suddenly turned towards him and there were angry shouts. His face had taken on a wild, insane look, and suddenly he had drawn his gun.

Several men charged towards him as he backed towards the door, but without hesitation he fired his gun into them, the sound hammering through the courtroom and bringing forth shouts and screams. The local blacksmith fell to the floor grasping his side. Steckline would have fired again and rushed from the courtroom, but another shot crashed out and the marshal went down, a large expanse of blood showing on his back where a bullet had passed through. Suddenly everyone's gaze swung to Seth Hardeman, who had risen to his unstable feet, a smoking revolver in his hand. He spoke but one word.

'Mavericker!'

Doctor Fischer had stooped over the fallen Steckline. When he straightened up, he said: 'Shot through the heart!'

He then turned his attention to the more important task of saving the life of the blacksmith whom Steckline had wounded. Fortunately his administrations were successful.

Kathleen was suddenly hugging Adam, unable to restrain her sobbing. Adam wanted to speak, to express his love for her, but he could not because he was too choked with emotion.

He was suddenly aware of a presence behind him. He turned to face his stepmother. There were tears glistening in her eyes, tears that he had never imagined her soul possessed. She reached out and took his hand in hers. 'I'm sorry, Adam,' she said in a strange cracked voice, 'sorry for everythin'.' And then she turned and was gone, helping her husband from the courtroom.

Seth Hardeman had done his duty that day, perhaps saved more than one life and the local community was grateful. His former health would never be restored. He would never be strong enough to run the ranch again. Soon he would ask Adam to take on the responsibility — but that would be a matter for Adam to discuss with Kathleen, because the future beckoned them and they had many things to ponder upon. Right now, Adam was released from his manacles and, arm in arm, he and Kathleen walked out into the Texas sunshine, knowing that whatever tragedies lay ahead, whatever challenges, they would face them together.

THE END

We do hope that you have enjoyed reading this large print book.

Did you know that all of our titles are available for purchase?

We publish a wide range of high quality large print books including:
Romances, Mysteries, Classics
General Fiction
Non Fiction and Westerns

Special interest titles available in large print are:
The Little Oxford Dictionary
Music Book, Song Book
Hymn Book, Service Book

Also available from us courtesy of Oxford University Press:
Young Readers' Dictionary
(large print edition)
Young Readers' Thesaurus
(large print edition)

For further information or a free brochure, please contact us at:
Ulverscroft Large Print Books Ltd.,
The Green, Bradgate Road, Anstey,
Leicester, LE7 7FU, England.
Tel: (00 44) **0116 236 4325**
Fax: (00 44) **0116 234 0205**

Other titles in the
Linford Western Library:

HIGH STAKES AT CASA GRANDE

T. M. Dolan

A gambler down on his luck, Latigo arrives in town bent on vengeance. His aim is to ruin Major Lonroy Crogan, the owner of the town of Casa Grande, and then to kill him. With a loaned poker stake, he soon makes enough money to threaten Crogan's empire by buying up property. However, danger lurks on the horizon and Latigo's plans seem doomed to failure. Will he be forced to flee Casa Grande as an all round loser?